Hello Mary

Thank-you so much for
letting us give a home to Tommy
and Jade. We are looking forward
to getting to know them.

I just wanted to share a verse
with you that was a precious
promise to me during some very
difficult times in my life. It
was a gem I discovered as I
was going through 1 & 2 Peter.

I. Peter 5:10
   And the God of all grace, who called
you to His eternal glory in Christ, after
you have suffered a little while
   WILL HIMSELF RESTORE you
and make you strong, firm, & steadfast.

Praying for you & your family.
Lee

Cowgirl Courage

J. H. Lee

WestBow
PRESS
A DIVISION OF THOMAS NELSON

WestBow Press books may be ordered through booksellers or by contacting:

WestBow Press
A Division of Thomas Nelson
1663 Liberty Drive
Bloomington, IN 47403
www.westbowpress.com
1-(866) 928-1240

ISBN: 978-1-4908-0590-0 (sc)
ISBN: 978-1-4908-0591-7 (hc)
ISBN: 978-1-4908-0589-4 (e)

Library of Congress Control Number: 2013915119

Printed in the United States of America.

WestBow Press rev. date: 09/12/2013

Dedication

To my daughters, who have taught me
to delight in the simple joys of life.

Table of Contents

CHAPTER 1

HEART HAMMERING AND LUNGS BURNING, BROOKE fought desperately to keep her slim lead. To lose a race to her younger sister would be disappointing, but to be defeated on her twelfth birthday? That would be worse than swallowing a mouthful of porcupine quills. If only she had four legs instead of two! Skye would be the one eating dust for a change.

Charging past their parents, Brooke could hear Skye's footsteps echoing her own as they churned up the gravel path toward the towering red barn. Success would be hers if she was the first to touch its rough, wooden wall. Only five more strides. Four. Three. Confident of her win, Brooke stretched out her left arm and glanced over her shoulder. To see the disbelief on Skye's face when she lost the race would be the icing on the cake.

"Hurray . . . aaahhh!" Brooke's shout of joy erupted into a cry of alarm as the ground disappeared from under her feet. A jolt of pain shot through her left shoulder as it found the ground and skidded through the loose rocks and sand. She hit the barn with a thud, but not before she caught a glimpse of Skye's fingertips touching first.

"Yes!" Skye exclaimed as she leaned against the barn, breathing hard.

Sitting up, Brooke saw the look of triumph on Skye's face. It wasn't hard to miss. She was practically glowing. Brooke looked away. Defeat had become the icing on her cake, and it wasn't very pleasant to swallow.

Skye stretched out her hand. "You okay?"

"I'm fine," Brooke muttered, attempting to keep the irritation out of her voice. It wasn't Skye's fault that she had longer legs. Mom kept encouraging her to be patient. In time she would get taller. Yeah, right! Somehow that knowledge did little to stop the jealousy that was creeping in. Skye seemed to breeze through life without any struggles. Ignoring her sister's offer of help, Brooke stood up as Mom and Dad reached the barn.

Dad inspected the ground. "Nice track, Brooke. Remind me to hire you if I need some ditches dug."

Brooke smiled. "I can think of less painful ways to move gravel." She tried not to flinch as Mom's fingers prodded her throbbing shoulder.

"That tender?" Mom asked.

"A little, but I'll be okay," Brooke insisted, rotating her shoulder to show she was fine. She wasn't about to let a little pain disrupt her twelfth birthday.

Dad turned toward the barn doors. "That's good to hear, because I'm not sure your present could wait for another day."

A shiver of anticipation shot through Brooke, wiping out the disappointment of the lost race. She had been eagerly awaiting this day. If her gift was what she was hoping for, this would be an unforgettable birthday.

Dad motioned for her to join him. "Well, come on over here. Let's see what's behind those barn doors."

Pebbles crunched under Brooke's feet as she walked to the front of the barn. Built by her Grandpa many years ago, the hip-roofed building was still used in the winter and spring months on the Silver Valley Ranch. With one thousand calves born each year, the newborns needed a dry place to hide out in case of bad weather. Once summer came, the cows and calves grazed in the lush pastures of the river valley. As it was now July, the barn stood empty, except for a few horses kept in for riding.

"C'mon, Dad. Open the doors, please!" Brooke pleaded as she paced back and forth, her excitement making it impossible to stand still.

"Are you ready, cowgirl?"

Dad's question halted Brooke in her tracks. Cowgirl? She had been that at one time, but now? She wasn't sure. So much had changed since . . . Brooke looked at her Dad with unseeing eyes as that dreadful day of four months ago replayed in her memory.

That horse ride had begun like so many others. Brooke and Skye had told Dad they were riding down to the cabin at the river. Then they saddled their horses and rode off. As they left the yard, Dad yelled out his usual, "Be safe, girls! Have you got a cell phone?" While cell reception was spotty in the river hills, the girls could always ride to the top of the hill to get a call out if necessary. Brooke remembered laughing. She and Skye had been riding before they could walk. The river hills were their second home, and they were on their trustworthy horses, Buckshot and Indee. What could go wrong?

Everything.

As they rode down the trail to the cabin, Brooke noticed that Buckshot's feet were slipping every few steps. The ground was slimy under the thin layer of new grass that was emerging after a long winter. As the trail grew steeper, it only got worse. Buckshot was sliding more than he was walking. Realizing the danger, she tried to stop Buckshot and turn him around, but it was too late. They were careening down the hill out of control. Brooke was frightened, but she was determined to find a way to stop. She stuck with Buckshot until the trail reached a narrow ledge bordered by one of the many limestone cliffs that peppered their river valley. Sensing what might happen, she threw herself out of the saddle to the uphill side of the trail. Tumbling to a stop, she looked with dread toward her struggling horse, only to see him somersault over the ledge.

"Buckshot, no!"

Brooke shook her head, interrupting the echoes of that moment and causing the scene to retreat from her mind. Since that day, she had been unable to sit on a horse for more than two minutes. Each time she tried, fear would come stampeding in and trample her determination to get back in the saddle. Some cowgirl she was. The only thing that kept her from giving up was her love of horses and the thought that, if she could just find the right horse, she would be able to give her fears a kick in the pants and send them flying for good. She had tried the horses at the ranch, but they were too old, too young, or just not a good fit for her. The right horse was like a comfortable pair of riding boots—hard to find and not so easy to replace.

"Happy Birthday, Brooke." Dad's voice broke through her troubled thoughts.

Brooke's excitement began to grow as she watched Dad and Mom grip the handles to open the barn doors. If her birthday present was what she was hoping for, this could be the start of regaining what she had lost. Brooke's heart thudded as the gap between the doors widened to reveal . . .

An empty halter and lead rope.

CHAPTER

2

BROOKE'S HEART FALTERED AS SHE GAZED in bewilderment at the black halter and lead rope dangling lifelessly from the wooden post. Was this a joke? Black was one of her favorite colors, but she didn't need another halter and rope. Seeing the pleased faces of her parents, Brooke tried to swallow her disappointment. "Um, thanks," she said halfheartedly. "They are really nice."

"They? Really nice?" Dad looked puzzled. "Don't you like her?"

Brooke shook her head in confusion. Dad never called a halter and lead rope "her." What was he talking about?

Dad's bushy eyebrows furrowed as he glanced at Brooke and then went into the barn. He picked up the halter, turned it over in his hands, and let it drop back against the post before disappearing into the dark interior of the barn.

Brooke watched Mom and Skye as they walked to the barn. They appeared to be as stunned as Dad by this turn of events. Joining them she asked, "What's going on?"

Mom shrugged her shoulders. "Believe it or not, we had a lovely new mare tied to this post for you. Evidently, she had other ideas that didn't include standing here and waiting for us. She must have rubbed her halter off."

Brooke picked up the empty halter and hung it over her elbow. Gripping the lead rope with both arms, she yanked hard to loosen the slipknot that held it to the post. Despite the dull pain in her left shoulder, she found herself smiling. She was going to have her own horse. They just had to find it first! Since the front doors had been closed, it shouldn't be too hard to locate her. Brooke coiled up the rope in her hands as she saw Dad return. She took a quick peek behind him, eager to see her new horse.

"Water disappearing. A missing horse. What's next?" Dad muttered as he stopped beside her. "I'm sorry, Brooke. I checked all the stalls and even the tack room. There is no sign of her."

Brooke peered into the shadows of the barn. Disappearing water? A missing horse? Had her horse run off with the water bucket? What was Dad talking about?

Dad continued. "I did find the back door open just wide enough for a horse to squeeze through. I think she must have gone outside in search of water."

Brooke's eyes widened in alarm. The pasture behind the barn had over thirty horses in it. Adding a new horse into a herd that size was like dropping a lit match on a pile of dry leaves.

Horses could be vicious toward any new arrival. They would chase, bite, and kick the new horse until it learned where it stood in the pecking order, which was usually at the bottom. It was far better to introduce the newcomer to a couple of horses first.

"Dad, we have to find her," Brooke pleaded. Pictures of a bruised and bleeding horse flashed through her mind.

Dad put his arm around her shoulders and reassured her. "Don't worry, Brooke. We'll find her."

Brooke barely held in a frustrated laugh. Don't worry? That would be tough. While she knew they would find her horse, she was concerned about the condition she would be in when they did. It only took one well-placed kick to break a horse's leg.

Dad began to give orders. "Skye, go with Mom and check the north side of the pasture. Brooke, you come with me. We'll check the watering hole on the south end. I suspect that is where she will be."

Thwack! Brooke dropped the halter and lead rope as she ran to the back of the barn and went outside. Shielding her eyes from the brilliant sunlight, she scanned the horizon, looking for a lone horse. There was a chance that her horse was somewhere else on the ranch. Since the ranch's yard sat on top of a hill, she had a clear view of the green pastures and emerald fields of hay that stretched all the way to the hills of the Silverton River.

Realizing she didn't have a description of her horse Brooke questioned, "Hey, Dad. What color is my horse?" When there was no answer, she looked over her shoulder and saw that Dad had already started down a dirt path to the watering hole. She darted to the left to follow him.

A sharp yelp sounded from around Brooke's feet.

Startled, Brooke glanced down and saw she had stepped on Tuffy's paw. Tuffy was the family's black and gold Corgi dog, who being longer than he was tall, was often underfoot.

"Sorry, boy." Brooke reached down to pat his head and then hurried after Dad. Tuffy followed in hot pursuit. For a small dog, he was never far from the action. He loved to chase anything that moved.

"Do you think my horse could have made it all the way to the river, Dad?" Brooke gasped as she struggled to catch her breath.

Dad pointed, and shook his head. "I don't think so. Judging by the dust cloud at the watering hole, something has the horses riled up. In all likelihood that is where she is. We'd better get down there."

With a fleeting wish for longer legs, Brooke half sprinted to keep up as she followed Dad down the pasture trail. When they stopped, she could see the watering hole better. The horses were dashing back and forth in a wild, deadly game of tag. The willow trees surrounding the pool of water stretched out their gnarled branches with leafy fingers, ready to snatch anything that got too close.

Brooke swallowed hard. "Dad, we've got to do something." She didn't want to lose another horse, but to enter that commotion on foot would be foolish. Maybe Dad could do something if he got his horse, Chocolate. As she turned to give a voice to her idea, Tuffy whizzed past her, charging into the confusion. It was impossible to see him in the puffs of gray cloud rising from the ground, but she could hear his forceful bark, first on one side and then the other. It wasn't long before he had the horses headed north in a charging stampede.

"That silly dog," Dad said. "He's going to get hurt one of these days, chasing those horses like that. But this will be one time I won't get after him. He's got them headed right to the corrals. That's the only place we'll be able to get your horse separated from them. C'mon, we'd better go help him."

Brooke was about to follow when a lone whinny from the watering hole caught her attention. "Dad, wait! There's still a horse down there." She ran down the hill, stopping as she came to the tangled maze of willow trees. Peering through the twisted branches, a swish of movement caught her eye. Fighting through limbs that smacked her back as she passed by and dodging roots that threatened to trip her, Brooke hurried through the web of trees.

"Whoa, girl," Brooke said in a low, calm voice when she spotted a caramel colored horse that stood in a thick clump of willow trees. The horse turned its head and nickered. The soft vibrating sound coming from the horse's throat told Brooke the horse was happy to see her. As Brooke brushed the black mane out of the way she noticed the white markings on its face. It looked like someone had taken a paint brush and dabbed a small white star between the horse's eyes and then added a miniature snow covered mountain to its nose. As she continued her observation, she saw that the horse was putting weight on all its legs. So why wasn't she moving? Brooke continued to rub the horse's head as she moved to the other side.

"Oh, no! How did you do that?" Brooke stared in disbelief. The horse was firmly wedged in the middle of the bushes. There was no way it could get free on its own. She tried to pull on the limbs of one tree to free the horse, but she didn't have enough strength. Taking a step back, Brooke saw that it would be impossible for her to get the horse free without more help. She would just need to wait for Dad, as she didn't want to leave the horse alone.

"I see it, but I don't believe it," Dad's voice broke into Brooke's troubled thoughts. "In all my years, I have never seen a horse get trapped in a tree." He chuckled, "Well, this isn't exactly how I planned it, Brooke, but here is your new horse. Her name is Jazz."

Her horse? Brooke looked at Jazz in surprise. She had been so intent on wanting to free the horse she had failed to realize it might be hers. Thankful to have found her horse unhurt, she began to stroke Jazz's mane. "Don't worry girl. We'll find a way to get you out." She frowned at the willows that were holding Jazz captive. "Any ideas, Dad? I tried to pull the trees away, but they were too big."

Dad shook his head. "I don't think I have any other choice."

"Can't you get her out?" A shiver of foreboding crept up Brooke's spine at the sight of Dad's grim expression and his ominous words. "What are you going to do?"

"I have to get my chainsaw," Dad said. "We'll have to cut her out of the tree."

CHAPTER 3

"A CHAINSAW? DAD, ARE YOU CRAZY?" Brooke shrieked, unable to stop the words of disbelief that tumbled out of her mouth. She had just found Jazz safe and unharmed. She could only imagine what might happen if Jazz panicked while Dad was cutting away the trees that held her captive.

Dad walked around the cluster of trees. "It's the only way. She's wedged in there too tight. Even if we had an army of people to pull all those trees out of the way, a branch could snap and puncture her side. We have to cut the trees at their base. A chainsaw is the only thing that will work." Dad put his arm around Brooke's shoulder. "Don't worry, honey. We'll get her out."

More annoyed than comforted, Brooke looked at Dad doubtfully. There were those words again: "Don't worry." She wondered how he would feel standing in her shoes right now. He would probably take it all in stride. Nothing seemed to cause him alarm. As for her, on the other hand . . . well, that was a different story. But there wasn't a lot she could do about the situation except go along with what he said. And she had to admit, the last time he had said those words, it had worked out. They had found Jazz. Hopefully this time would end just as well.

"Hey! You guys in there?" Skye's voice echoed through the bushes.

"Yeah!" Dad shouted back. "Come in. We're on the left side of the watering hole."

The swishing of branches and snapping of twigs were the only sounds Brooke heard as she stood and rubbed Jazz's neck. Finally, Mom and Skye broke through the jungle of trees.

Mom walked toward Brooke. "Oh, good, you found her! We wondered what was happening when we saw our mighty Tuffy chasing the horses across the field, but you were nowhere in sight. Did Dad tell you who this is?"

Brooke opened her mouth to answer, but Dad interrupted, "Yes, I did. There is just one problem. Jazz is stuck in these trees. I need my chainsaw so we can get her out."

Mom's eyebrows rose. "A chainsaw? Really? Wouldn't a handsaw be better?"

Inwardly Brooke cheered, liking Mom's idea much better. A chainsaw seemed too loud, too big, too sharp, and too dangerous.

Dad shook his head. "It would take too long to cut away all these trees with a handsaw, and we need to free her quickly." He motioned to Skye, "Why don't you come with me and grab her halter and lead rope."

After Dad and Skye left, Brooke continued to rub Jazz's neck. "Hang on, girl. We'll get you out of there," she murmured. Jazz let out another soft nicker. Brooke leaned her forehead against Jazz's head. She hadn't known Jazz for long, but she was beginning to love this horse already. Not only did she seem to understand Brooke's words, but it was clear she had a quiet nature for she wasn't in a state of panic in her confinement.

Mom knelt down and began to pull at some of the smaller branches that were tangled around Jazz's legs. "So, do you like her?"

"I do. She's calm and pretty, not to mention smart. Not many horses can get out of a halter and then squeeze through a barn door to go in search of water."

Mom laughed. "Well, I don't know if I would call that smart. Look where it got her."

"Yeah, I suppose," Brooke giggled. "But it shows that she can think and figure things out. That's what made Buckshot such a good horse. We could work together as a team. I didn't always have to be showing him what to do."

"Do you still miss him?"

"Yeah, but I miss riding even more. Every time I get on a horse, the panic that grips me overpowers any desire to ride." Brooke's shoulders sagged as she combed the tangles out of Jazz's mane with her fingers. Would she ever ride again?

"Well, that's why we bought Jazz for you," Mom said. "She's quiet, smart, and reliable. Not to mention sure-footed. She was raised in the river hills. When Dad tried her out at a ranch downriver from here, he was extremely impressed."

Brooke stopped combing Jazz's mane and looked her in the eyes. There she saw a kindness that gave her hope. Perhaps with Jazz she would once again have a trusted partner that she would enjoy riding with.

When Dad and Skye returned, Skye gave the black halter and lead rope to Brooke. Brooke slipped the halter over Jazz's head and buckled it up while Dad took the chainsaw out of its bright orange case.

He pointed to a spot about fifteen feet ahead of them. "I'm going to start the chainsaw over there so she won't get too startled when the engine begins running. Once she seems okay with it, I will walk up to her and start sawing. Keep her focus on you, and talk to her. If she panics when she sees the sawdust flying out to the sides, cover her eyes. That will help her not to get spooked. Ready?"

Brooke nodded and gripped the lead rope so tight her knuckles turned white. She jumped as the chainsaw rumbled to life, spewing out blue-grey smoke. With each rev of the engine, Brooke's heart raced a little more. She looked at Jazz. Her ears were perked forward as she watched the chainsaw, but amazingly she didn't seem overly concerned about it.

"I think you should let me hold her," Skye yelled over the noise of the chainsaw as Dad walked past. "You're as white as a ghost. You look like you're going to faint." She held out her hand to take the rope.

"I'm fine," Brooke blurted with aggravation. Jazz was hers, and she was going to be the one to stand with her in this.

Brooke's breathing quickened as the engine accelerated and the chain spun into action. The blade reached for the first willow tree and with the contact, sawdust sprayed in every direction. Jazz's head flew up as the first tree fell away. She snorted and stamped her foot, showing her irritation. With that, the edges of Brooke's vision turned black and the world started to spin. She felt as though she were going to topple like that tree. Dropping the rope, she backed up until she found a tree to lean on.

Brooke watched in dismay as Skye stepped in and picked up the rope. As she rubbed Jazz's head, it slowly came down until it rested in her hand. Brooke tried to step forward and take the rope, but as soon as she moved the whole world seemed to twist sideways. She closed her eyes to regain her balance. How did Skye do it? Even in tense situations, she seemed fearless, always able to do what needed to be done. Brooke was thankful that Skye was there to help, but at the same time she felt a tad jealous.

"Okay! That should do it," Dad yelled as he shut off the chainsaw. "Lead her out!"

Brooke opened her eyes and noticed that Dad had cut most of the trees to the right of Jazz. The ground was crisscrossed with fallen limbs.

She stepped forward to take the rope from Skye. "Thanks," Brooke said. Skye nodded and backed out of the way.

Brooke tugged on the rope, and Jazz stepped forward, free of her willow prison. Relieved, Brooke put her arms around Jazz's neck. What a birthday it had been so far!

And the day was only half done.

C H A P T E R

4

"I CAN HONESTLY SAY THAT IS the first time I have opened a birthday present that was wrapped up in a tree," Dad chuckled as he knelt down to put the chainsaw back into its case.

Brooke looked over at him. "And it wasn't even yours!"

"Right! I did all the work, while you get the fun of having her. We'll have to work something out." Dad paused. "How about you promise to keep her from wedging herself into any more trees?"

"Hopefully that won't be too hard!" Brooke agreed as she stared into the chocolate marble swirl of Jazz's eyes. "Did you hear that? No more trees!" she chided. She had a feeling that life with Jazz would be like those Christmas candies Mom made. They were enjoyable, but there were often some unexpected surprises waiting inside.

"Sounds like a plan," Dad replied. "Now, why don't we get ourselves out of this tangled wood?" He turned and left the thicket.

"Hey, Brooke, do you want to go for a ride when we get back?" Skye called over her shoulder. "I want to stretch Indee's legs before the cattle drive tomorrow. It would be a good chance to try out Jazz."

Brooke hesitated before answering. Every year, she and Skye would help move the last of the cows and calves to the river hills and then spend a week at their cabin by the river with Dad. They would look after the cattle while the ranch workers took a well-deserved vacation. If she wanted to be of any help tomorrow and the rest of the week, she would need to be riding Jazz. Chasing cows on foot? That was better left for the dogs. "Um, sure, let's go," she said as she tugged on Jazz's rope and fell in line behind Skye. Agreeing in word was the easy part. She would have to muster a lot of courage to put those words into action.

"Before you girls go riding, make sure to give Jazz some water and hay," Dad said.

"And since we missed lunch with our adventure, you need to have a bite to eat as well," Mom added.

"Hopefully she means something other than hay," Skye half-whispered back to Brooke.

Brooke barely contained a burst of laughter as she stepped out of the willows. Count on Skye to say something like that. She urged Jazz to walk faster and caught up to Skye. "Well, you know Dad is always saying hay is healthy."

"For cows and horses."

"I remember one time you picked a few alfalfa plants and asked Mom to put them in pancakes." Brooke teased. "Mom was confused. She looked at you and asked if you were sure that was what you wanted."

"I did not," Skye protested.

"You did too. That night we had nice pancakes with chopped green alfalfa bits in them. And you know, they didn't taste half bad, with enough syrup on them. So maybe a little hay with a little syrup . . ." Brooke let the idea float in the air.

"Yuck!" Skye grimaced. "Pancakes with syrup is one thing, but hay with syrup? That would be nasty."

"Some horses would probably like it. They eat sugar cubes."

"Horses, yes. But, as far as I know, I do not have a mane and tail."

"Are you sure?" Brooke took a quick peek behind Skye. "You might have something hanging out the back of your jeans."

Skye spun a frantic circle. "I do not!"

"So why did you look?" Brooke snickered as Skye scrunched up her face and stuck out her tongue. Sometimes it was so easy to get a reaction out of her sister. For one who was so fast on her feet, she could quite easily be tripped up in a battle of wits.

Brooke was still chuckling as they walked up to the barn. As she entered, the sunlight faded into a sea of gray. Behind her, she could hear Jazz testing the air, sniffing at the jumble of smells that were concealed in the old building.

"The only light switch is at the other end of the barn. We have to walk through," Brooke explained softly as she led Jazz through the murky darkness. "There's nothing to feeee . . . Ah!" She jumped back in alarm as the shadowy silhouette of a horse head flitted toward them over a stall gate, snorting into the air with interest.

Brooke let out a relieved sigh. "Easy, Chocolate. It's me." She stepped forward to pet Dad's horse, but he had no interest in her. Jazz had all of his attention. The two horses stood nose to nose, smelling each other. It was an odd way to get acquainted, but it worked for horses. She couldn't help but think of what would happen if she stepped up to a stranger, sniffed her, and used her odor as a gauge to decide if she wanted to be friends. Brooke laughed inwardly. In some cases, it might not be a bad idea.

"Well, Jazz, now that you've made a new friend, let's put you away." She led Jazz to the end of the barn, flipped on the lights, and put her into the empty stall that was by the door. She unhooked the lead rope and closed the gate.

"Now, the question is, will you stay in there?" Brooke looked at the rope latch that slipped over the top of the stall gate to hold it closed. If Jazz was determined to get out, that would be easy to open. With one flip of her nose, she would be able to nudge the rope off and be free to go wherever she pleased. A secondary lock would be a good idea. Kneeling down, she wove the lead rope back and forth between the door and the stall.

"What are you doing?"

Brooke started slightly at the sound of Skye's voice behind her. "Making sure my horse doesn't escape again." Brooke stepped back to admire the serpentine lock she had made. "Think that will hold her?" she asked. As she turned to look at Skye, she was surprised by a tangled mass of hay swishing past her head.

"I brought her the hay, but if you want syrup, you'll have to get that yourself," Skye joked as she leaned the pitchfork against the barn wall.

Brooke listened as Jazz crunched the green stems between her teeth. "She seems to like it just the way it is. I'll get her some water, and we should be done."

"Good. I'm hungry enough to eat a horse!"

"Or some hay?" Brooke jested. She hurried to the tack room, found the silver water pail, and placed it under the tap. As the rush of water splattered her with little droplets, she recalled Dad's words about disappearing water. Obviously this water wasn't missing. What had he meant? Once the pail was full, she returned to the stall and poured the sloshing liquid into the rubber water tub. "She must not have had much time to drink at the water hole," Brooke commented, watching as Jazz guzzled the water with deep gulps.

"Of course not! She was too tied up," Skye quipped. "C'mon. If we hang around here much longer, there won't be much time left for a ride."

"Sure, let's go." Brooke followed Skye out of the barn. As she walked into the sunshine, fear and doubt trailed after her like two pesky mosquitoes. Giving Jazz food and water was the easy part. She only wished riding her would be just as simple. The accident with Buckshot had rattled her nerves to the point she was not only scared to get on a horse, but she also doubted her ability to ride. She couldn't shake the thought that if she would have taken different steps that day, things would have turned out differently.

Brooke looked back at the barn and thought of the caramel colored horse inside. If any horse could help her conquer these fears she had, it would be Jazz. But Jazz could only do so much. Brooke knew she would have to confront and conquer her own doubts.

That would take courage.

Something she was desperately seeking and still had to find.

CHAPTER

5

"WOULD YOU HURRY UP?" SKYE'S IRRITATED voice lashed through the air like a whip.

Brooke nodded her head, unable to open her mouth to answer. Her mouth was stuffed with roast beef and bread. She tried to swallow, but her sandwich was stuck in her mouth like glue. Even smothering her meat in ketchup hadn't helped. Taking little sips of water as she chewed her mouthful, she moistened the lump that resembled cement until it sluggishly made its way down to her stomach.

"I'm done," Brooke choked out. Unable to eat the last half of her sandwich, she set it down on her plate. She took another swallow of water and brushed the crumbs from her hands.

"I'll be at the barn, getting ready," Skye said impatiently, slamming the door as she went outside.

Brooke stood up and carried her plate and cup to the kitchen sink. "Thanks, Mom."

"Is that all you want?"

"Yeah. I'm not that hungry." It felt like there were two cats viciously scrapping in her stomach. Mixing food into that restlessness hadn't been a good idea.

"Well, I hope you feel like eating by supper. We're having steak, baked potatoes, and Black Forest cake for dessert."

"Mmm—sounds good." Brooke pasted a smile on her face, although the thought of all her favorite foods did little to calm the nervousness she was feeling.

Walking to the entry, Brooke peeked out the open window. Noticing that Skye was already halfway to the barn, she tugged on her black riding boots and went outside. As she walked, the tangled knots in her stomach began to unwind. It was a beautiful day for a ride. The sunlight shimmered on the leaves as a light breeze caused them to frolic to and fro. The gentle wind teased her hair, causing the long blonde strands to flutter across her face and tickle her nose.

"Skye," Brooke called ahead. "I have to grab a ponytail elastic for my hair. I'll be right back." She didn't want her hair to cloud her vision while she was riding.

"An elastic? I've got an extra." Skye came back and rolled up the sleeve of her blue western shirt, showing off a selection of hair elastics on her wrist. "I always carry a few with me. What color?"

"It doesn't matter," Brooke said, "As long as it keeps my hair under control."

"Colors have different meanings, you know." Skye remarked. She pulled a fluorescent pink one off her wrist and handed it to Brooke. "How about this one?"

"And what does pink mean?" Brooke teased as she turned into the wind so the breeze would blow the strands of hair away from her face.

"Friendship."

Brooke gathered her circus of flying hair and secured it at the back of her neck. "Well, thanks," she stated, turning back to face Skye, but she had already left. Walking toward the barn, she thought about what Skye had said, and she had to admit Skye's color choice was a good one. Sometimes as sisters they were rivals, and other times they were foes, but through it all they remained friends.

Brooke entered the barn, surprised at the shadows that greeted her. A small shiver trembled up her spine as she reached for the light switch. Something wasn't right.

"Boo!"

Brooke's heart leaped within her, pulling her feet off the ground. She whirled around at the sound of snickering behind her, knowing immediately who the culprit was.

"Skye!"

"You looked so funny! And for a second, you were almost as tall as me." Skye continued to laugh as she turned around and walked further into the barn.

Dad walked into the barn and flipped on the lights. "Is everything okay?"

"Just fine," Brooke muttered through tense lips, all thoughts of friendship vanishing. There were times being a sister was a trial. Usually Skye's capers didn't annoy her so much, but today her nerves were already stretched past their limit.

"Okay. I'll be outside getting things organized for the cattle drive tomorrow." Dad started to leave, but then turned back and added, "Make sure you come and see me before you leave for your ride."

Taking a deep breath to calm her nerves, Brooke unlaced her makeshift lock and led Jazz out of the stall. Tying her to a post, she glanced over Jazz's back and watched as Skye brushed her tall black gelding. Indee laid his ears back and threatened to nip at her as she reached under him and brushed toward his back legs. They were a good match, Brooke thought. Each one was unpredictable at times.

"Can you pass me your brush once you're finished?" Brooke asked.

"I'm done. Catch." Skye tossed the brush through the air and it landed in Brooke's hands with a smack.

"Are you ready for this ride? I hope I am," Brooke murmured as she brushed the remnants of sawdust and twigs out of Jazz's black mane. If only horses could talk. She would explain her doubts and ask Jazz to be calm and patient with her as she rebuilt her confidence.

Once she finished brushing Jazz, Brooke went to the tack room to get her saddle and bridle. Walking toward the ten foot saddle tree, she spun its trunk until the branch with her saddle on it was in front of her. With three levels of branches for holding saddles, Brooke was glad hers was on the bottom row. She placed her hands under the saddle horn and the back of the seat. Taking a deep breath she heaved it up into her arms. Wedging her way through the tack room door, she saw a sight that made her drop her saddle and run.

"Oh, no! Not again! Jazz, stop! Whoa, girl!" Jazz was tugging on the end of the lead rope with her teeth. She had nearly loosened the knot that held her captive to the post, and the barn doors stood wide open.

"You untie ropes too?" Brooke questioned in disbelief. She pulled the rope from Jazz's teeth. What was she going to do now? Jazz's skills for escaping seemed limitless. She thought a moment and then remembered a trick Dad had shown her. She looped the rope around the post and tied it back to the halter. With the knot under Jazz's chin, her teeth couldn't reach it. "That should hold you," she said with satisfaction, and hurried back to get her saddle.

"I am glad you are not tall. It makes it easier to get your tack on," Brooke commented, centering a striped blanket on Jazz's back. She swung the saddle on and reached under Jazz's stomach to do up the cinches, pulling the slack out of the straps until the saddle was secure. Jazz stood calmly while she removed the halter and fit the bridle onto her head. Taking the reins into her hand, she led Jazz out of the barn.

Skye joined them outside. "Wow! If your horse were any shorter, Indee would be able to step right over her."

Observing that the top of her saddle horn sat about eight inches below the one on Indee's back, Brooke remarked, "Just because you have a gigantic gelding doesn't mean mine is short. I prefer to think of her as . . ." She paused to think of the right word. "Refined."

"Refined, hey? Well, refined as she may be, you may want to pack your puddle boots for our campout."

Brooke glanced at the green grass and pebbles around the barn. There wasn't a puddle in sight. "And why is that?"

"The river is always high this time of the year with the melting snow from the mountains. We will be crossing it many times while we look after the cows. While my feet are staying nice and dry on my giant, you are going to be swimming with your refined mare."

"Well, you . . ." Brooke began to respond but was interrupted as Dad walked up.

"Have you two decided where you are riding?"

Brooke glanced at Skye and shrugged her shoulders. Their ranch covered 10,000 acres, and for safety, Dad wanted to know their riding plans. That way, if they got into trouble or didn't return in time, he would know where to start looking for them.

"Let's ride along the top of the river hills," Skye suggested.

Brooke sucked in a startled breath. The river hills used to be her favorite place to ride, but she hadn't been back there since the accident. What was Skye thinking?

Dad looked at his watch. "Okay. Try and be back here by five-thirty. You wouldn't want to be late for your birthday supper." He gave Brooke's shoulder a squeeze. "Have fun on Jazz. We chose her because we were confident she would be a good horse for you."

Brooke nodded, wishing she could grab hold of that confidence. She could feel her panic rising. Taking a deep breath, she fought to push her troublesome thoughts to the back of her mind. Enough was enough. It was time to take action on the fact that Jazz was a quiet horse with a good mind. She had seen the truth of that today.

Brooke took a hold of the reins and put her left foot up into the stirrup. For a fleeting second, she had a ridiculous urge to ask for someone to put glue on her saddle so that once she was on she would have to stick to it. She shut her eyes for a moment. She had lost so much, but today was the first step in moving forward. She would face this, and she would win.

She had no choice. If she wanted to ride again, she had to stay on.

There was no other way.

CHAPTER

6

SITTING IN THE SADDLE, BROOKE RESISTED the impulse to climb back down. She gritted her teeth and pretended that she really was stuck to the saddle. Leaning forward to rub Jazz's neck, she reminded herself of the facts. Jazz was a good horse. She was reliable. She could be trusted. Now it was time to act on that trust.

"Let's go," Brooke said, amazed at the strength of her voice. She was determined to do this, one small step at a time. She picked up the reins and squeezed Jazz's sides with her legs, giving Jazz the cue to walk. Immediately, Jazz stepped forward and started down the driveway. Skye rode beside her on Indee. The eight hooves of the two horses sounded like an odd set of drums. Jazz's hooves clomped steadily, while Indee provided the offbeat as he pranced slowly on the gravel.

"Hey, Brooke. Wanna race and see how fast your horse is?" Skye asked.

Brooke gulped. She thought hard to come up with a good reason not to race.

"Um, let's just walk," she said, hoping she didn't sound like a scared chicken. "Since it's my first ride on Jazz, I'd like to keep it slow for today." She was relieved when Skye nodded her head in agreement. Maybe if the ride went well, Brooke would suggest they trot part of the way home.

Brooke began to relax as they rode through the flowering purple of the alfalfa fields to the hills that framed the Silverton River. Their ranch—the Silver Valley Ranch—took its name from this river. Brooke gazed down into the green valley that was dotted with several black cows and their calves. The limestone cliffs that speckled the hills gleamed white in the afternoon sun.

"Look over there!" Skye said, pointing to her left. "Some of the calves are playing tag!"

Brooke watched as a quartet of adventurers ran across a small meadow. As they raced away from their mothers, they were joined by more calves. "They look silly when they run around with their tails straight up in the air like that."

"Like miniature flags running around on four legs."

Brooke watched the calves play for a few minutes and then let her gaze wander to the curves and bends of the river far below. The river was peaceful, but something was missing.

"Skye, do you hear that?" Brooke asked.

Skye was silent before she answered. "No, I don't hear anything but the odd cow mooing."

"Doesn't it seem too quiet? This time of year we can usually hear the roaring of the swollen river all the way to our house. We should easily hear it from this spot." Brooke's curiosity grew as she looked at the river glittering in the afternoon sun. Could this have something to do with the "water disappearing" Dad had mentioned?

"Well, I guess if the river's lower you won't have to worry about your feet getting wet on your short horse!" Skye teased. "C'mon. Let's ride a ways."

Brooke rode beside Skye as they wound their way through the wild grass that waved gently along the top of the river hills. The fingers of the wind tugged on the manes of the horses, making their hair dance in the breeze.

Brooke lost track of time as they walked along the banks of the river. She was startled when Skye's voice broke the silence.

"We'd better turn around if we are going to be back in time for your birthday supper."

Turning Jazz toward home, Brooke realized she was sad to leave the river. Spending time there had reawakened her love for riding and had given her some good memories to replace the bad ones. She glanced at Skye, remembering it had been her idea to ride here. Maybe in her own way she was trying to help, and it seemed to be working.

"Do you want to try trotting?" Skye asked.

Brooke thought a moment. Jazz was relaxed and she responded to the cues she was given. What could go wrong?

In answer to Skye's question, Brooke squeezed Jazz's sides with her legs, and she quickened her steps into a trot. The gentle up-down motion was a huge difference from Buckshot. When he trotted, she had felt like a dull nail being hammered into a board. She was also pleased to see that Jazz kept pace with Indee, even when his step became more energetic.

"Indee really wants to go. Would you mind if we ran a little ways?" Skye requested.

Run? Brooke thought she was doing well at a trot, but she didn't want Jazz to go any faster.

"No, but go ahead if you want to," Brooke said. She could tell Skye was fighting hard to hold Indee in. She was going to ask Skye to allow her to get Jazz stopped before she ran off, but she never had the chance. Skye leaned low in the saddle and made a kissing sound with her lips to cue Indee into a run. Indee leaped forward, and Jazz took off like a shot beside him. The force of her start caught Brooke off guard and almost threw her backwards out of the saddle. Brooke fought to keep her balance. Gripping the saddle with her knees, she put both reins into her right hand and reached ahead to grab the saddle horn so she could pull herself forward.

"Whoa, Jazz! Whoa!" Brooke yelled. Jazz and Indee sprinted side by side, matching each other's speed. Brooke had to stop Jazz. This was not what she had planned. Forcing her feet forward in her stirrups, she leaned back in the saddle. By applying firm, steady pressure to the reins with both hands, Brooke felt Jazz cut back her speed. Indee bounded ahead as Jazz continued to slow down, but that didn't last for long. The rein in Brooke's left hand snapped in two. Jazz shot ahead, eating up the ground between her and Indee. Brooke dropped the useless piece of leather and clawed at the saddle horn to regain her balance.

The drumming of the horses' hooves as they thundered across the ground matched the pounding of Brooke's heart. She was on a runaway horse racing across an open field with only one rein.

How would she ever stop?

CHAPTER 7

As Jazz flew across the field Brooke clung to her saddle, wondering for a moment if this is how an ant would feel clinging to dandelion fuzz as it swooped through the air. She was thankful that her runaway mount was shadowing Indee, so at least in a small way, their direction was controlled. But quick on the heels of any reassurance that notion may have brought came pure panic! How was she ever going to stop with only one rein? Frantic ideas whirled through her thoughts, until her mind snatched at one that might just work. If Skye could get Indee to remove his hooves from the gas pedal, so to speak, maybe Jazz would follow his example.

"Skye, stop!" Brooke yelled, but the air snatched her words and carried them away before they were heard. Her lips tightened together as she considered the thirty foot gap between them. She had to get closer. That was the only way Skye would hear her plea for help. Feeling somewhat like a bee chasing after an eagle, Brooke leaned forward and squeezed the saddle tightly with her legs. She didn't know if her little mare could catch up, but she had to try.

"Heeyah!" she urged. Jazz's left ear flickered back and then forward. Brooke grasped the saddle horn as Jazz found another gear and surged ahead. Little by little she ate up the distance between her and Indee. Waiting until they were side by side, Brooke called out, "Skye, stop! My rein broke!" She frantically waved her single rein in the air. If Skye couldn't comprehend her words, hopefully she would be able to perceive what the problem was through her actions.

Keeping her body low over the saddle, Brooke glanced out of the corner of her eye. She saw Indee resist the pull of the reins, tossing his head as he fought to keep running. Skye persisted however, and gradually he began to gear down. Brooke drew in a quick breath of relief. The first part of her plan was successful. Hopefully the second part would work as well. She waited with each hoof beat for Jazz's stride to shorten and slow.

Brooke's relief was short-lived. The ground continued to whiz past in a blur. At this speed, they would soon reach the line where the hay field ended and the cow pasture started. That line was marked with a barbed wire fence meant to protect the growing feed crop from cattle who would love to eat the fresh forage. Brooke knew if they ran through the wire, there could be serious injury to them both. The sharp barbs would shred Jazz's hide, and if the cuts were deep, they could turn deadly due to loss of blood or infection. Brooke felt her heart shudder.

She had already lost Buckshot. She couldn't lose Jazz. She had to get her turned around. But how?

She glanced at her single rein. It was the only tool she had. As they continued to rush toward the fence, an idea began to take shape in her mind. Horses could not run at full speed in a tight circle. If she could get Jazz circling, she might be able to slow her down.

Slightly shifting her weight into the right stirrup, Brooke pulled lightly on the right rein. Jazz arched her head to the right, and her shoulder followed as she leaned into the circle. Brooke maintained steady, light pressure on the rein. If she applied too much force she would pull Jazz off balance, and they would both crash to the ground.

"What are you doing?" Skye's voice rang out.

Brooke didn't answer as she and Jazz flew past Indee and Skye in a wide loop. Gradually Jazz cut back her speed to a gallop, then a lope and finally a trot as Brooke spiraled her into a tighter and tighter circle. Now that the pace had slackened, Brooke guided Jazz's head closer to her right stirrup. In this way she could apply "the brakes." Jazz continued to corkscrew until her back feet were pivoting around her front. Finally she stopped.

Brooke drew in a shuddering breath as a wave of relief poured over her. Disaster had been averted. Her plan had worked. She released the tension from the rein, and reached down to rub Jazz's sweaty neck. What a ride!

Skye came alongside them. "I thought you said you didn't want to run."

"I didn't," Brooke gasped, trying to catch her breath. Her heart was pounding so rapidly, she felt as if she had been the one sprinting across the field. "I was going to ask you to wait until I had Jazz stopped before you took off, but you left before I had the chance. When Indee bolted, Jazz leaped forward so fast she almost threw me out of the saddle."

"Why didn't you stop her? I heard you shout 'Stop!' and then you went flying past. I thought you were trying to trick me so you could win the race."

Brooke showed Skye all that remained of her left rein.

"Your rein broke? No wonder she wouldn't stop." Skye paused and then said, "We can't fix that out here. How are you going to get home?"

Brooke gazed at the ranch yard. It was still a good distance away. The log house appeared to be little more than a dollhouse and the forty foot poplar trees that bordered the driveway looked as if they could be picked for a bouquet of flowers. What could she do? She could try to ride back with one rein, but she didn't want to risk another runaway. Once was enough. She could lead Jazz, but her legs were quivering so much, she wasn't sure they would have the strength to stand, let alone walk that distance.

Brooke eyed the lead rope bobbing back and forth as Indee tossed his nose up and down against the bees that buzzed around his head. Skye had left Indee's halter and rope on under his bridle. Although they often did this so they could tie up their horses if needed, Brooke had left Jazz's at the barn, thinking she wouldn't need it on this short ride. How wrong she had been. Thankfully though, she could use Indee's.

Brooke voiced her idea. "Skye, can I use your lead rope?"

"My lead rope? Sure, I guess." Untwisting the purple and black striped rope from her saddle horn, Skye slid out of the saddle and unclipped the other end from Indee's halter.

"Here you go," she said, handing it up to Brooke.

"Since you are down there, could you clip it onto the bridle?" Brooke questioned, unsure if her trembling legs would hold her up. If she got out of the saddle and fell to the ground, Skye would make sure she never forgot it. She was relieved when Skye attached the rope to the metal ring of Jazz's bit and handed the end of the rope up to her. She had two reins again.

"That's a good idea," Skye commented as she climbed back onto Indee. "If there is more trouble on the way home, you will be ready."

Brooke agreed. "That's the plan. They are not the most stylish, but they should get me home."

"Maybe you should start a new trend. You could call them Rainbow Reins."

"They are colorful, but I think I will stick with the leather ones." Brooke picked up her left rein and turned Jazz toward home. "We'd better get back. Dad will soon be wondering where we are."

As they walked home, Brooke pondered over what had just happened. She couldn't understand why Jazz had dashed across the field like a mad bull and then responded so well to the cues she was given to slow down. It didn't make sense. She wasn't hotheaded. Even after that long run, she walked calmly beside a prancing Indee.

"Jazz is quick for a short horse," Skye remarked.

"She can hustle when she wants to. I wonder what she would do in a real race," Brooke speculated out loud, even though racing Jazz was not something she was going to attempt at any point in the near future.

Skye scowled. "She might even be faster than Indee."

Brooke chuckled at the grimace on Skye's face. It appeared that the thought of her giant steed being outrun by a midget horse was hard to swallow.

Back at the barn, Brooke unsaddled Jazz and rubbed her down. Feeling the heat radiating from Jazz's hide, Brooke decided to return later to give her a drink. Cold water in the stomach of a hot horse was not a good idea as it could cause cramps. She put Jazz in her stall and then topped up her hay so she would have enough for the night.

Walking to the house, Brooke felt her stomach rumble as the delicious scent from the barbeque tingled her nose. "Mmm—that smell's good," she said as her mouth began to water.

"It does, and I'm hungry. Last one to the house does the dishes," Skye taunted as she ran past.

Brooke shook her head as she recaptured a few strands of hair that had escaped from the pink elastic Skye had given her. Some things didn't change. Skye was like a pinball, ricocheting from one thing to the next. Climbing up the steps to the deck, she watched as Dad flipped the steaks over. An orange flash shot up as the juices dripped down on the hot coals.

"Hey, birthday girl! How was your day?" Dad called over his shoulder.

Brooke joined him on the deck, unsure of how to describe it. It had been exciting to receive Jazz for a birthday present, but alarming to find her stuck in some trees. It had been difficult to climb onto Jazz's back, but rewarding to take the first step in conquering her fears. Even the terrifying horse race had turned out alright, and it had helped her gain confidence that she could make the right decision and put it into action in a dangerous situation.

And then there was Skye.

At times she had been more than a little irritated with her, but Brooke realized she owed her a thank-you. It was Skye who pushed her to ride to the river for the first time since the accident, and it had been pleasant to ride along the hills again. She now had some good memories to replace the bad. As she continued to think about her day, she realized there was only one word to describe it.

"Unforgettable."

Dad slathered some barbeque sauce onto the steaks. "Unforgettable? That is an interesting word to describe a birthday. Hopefully you mean that in a good way." Dad smiled. "And how was Jazz?"

"I like her," Brooke replied, although she still had some questions. Almost everything that happened today proved that Jazz was a calm, gentle minded and well trained horse. But Brooke could not understand why Jazz had bolted like a bullet shot out of a gun when Indee took off. If that was how she responded to another horse running alongside her, what would she do at the round up tomorrow? Cattle drives could be wild.

Cows and calves would be charging to and fro to find each other, and the horses, guided by their riders, would be running back and forth to stop any runaways.

What would happen if Jazz went crazy in all the chaos?

CHAPTER 8

"HELLO. ANYONE HOME?"

A distant voice tickled the edges of Brooke's dream-filled mind. She struggled to make sense of the words. Surely it couldn't be morning. The alarm clock had not rung.

"Hey, are you planning to spend the whole day in bed?"

Brooke rolled onto her back. Just like a mosquito, the irritating voice wasn't going away. She tried to open her eyelids but they were glued shut with the heaviness of sleep.

Suddenly, a soft but firm thump hit Brooke across the chest and then lifted. As she blindly raised herself up onto her elbows, her head made contact with the attacker. Brooke opened her eyes to stark blackness, but that lasted for only a moment. The cloud lifted and Brooke saw Skye's sly smile as she gripped her pillow. Brooke threw both hands up to block the feather missile as it flew down for another strike.

"I'm up. I'm up," Brooke rasped, still not awake. She cleared her throat to free it from the frogs that had taken up residence there in the night.

Skye pushed Brooke's feet out of the way and flopped down onto the end of the bed. "Are you going to sleep all day?" she teased.

"What time is it?" Brooke rubbed her eyes, and then wished she hadn't. They felt like sandpaper.

"It's time to get up!" Skye took hold of the pillow, jumped up, and threw it once more.

Trying to duck, Brooke slipped off the side of her bed and crashed to the floor. Snatching her pillow she fired it at Skye who darted out of the way. The pillow sailed out the door and into the hallway.

Yelp! A sharp bark came from Tuffy as the pillow of fluff hit him on the nose. A fierce growl came from his throat. He half-crouched and stared at the pillow, as if expecting it to attack him again.

"Hey, what's going on up there? Are you girls getting ready?" Dad's voice boomed up the oak stairwell. "We've got a big day ahead of us. Hurry it up. Jim and Joe are already gathering the cows."

"Oh man, the cattle drive," Brooke exclaimed. With the all commotion, she had forgotten about it.

Skye tossed her pillow onto the bed. "I guess we better put this pillow fight on hold."

"Yeah, Dad sounds like he wants to get going." Brooke slipped into her denim jeans and long-sleeved cotton shirt.

They would protect her legs and arms from sunburn and any scrapes she might get while riding through trees. She ran a brush through her hair and looked for something to tie it back into a ponytail.

"Can I use your elastic again?" Brooke asked as she snatched it from the night table that was next to her bed.

"Sure. Keep it. I have lots more."

Brooke twisted the pink band around her hair and slipped down to the washroom to clean up. She was in the middle of brushing her teeth when she heard Skye taunt, "Last one to the kitchen has to do the dishes!"

"Wat's ot air!" Brooke tried to holler, but her words got tangled up with the bubbles that were spewing from her mouth. She spit them out and rinsed with water. "That's not fair!" she yelled more clearly this time. Wiping her mouth on her shirt sleeve, she dashed out the door and down the stairs even though she already knew this was another race she had lost.

Brooke slid into her seat at the table. "Wow, Mom. This looks good." Two eggs, four slices of bacon, and two pieces of toast filled her plate. A jar of homemade raspberry jam sat in the middle of the table. It was a big breakfast, but she knew she would be thankful for it once she was on the cattle drive. Her fork plinked her plate as she cut into her eggs, causing the yellow yolks to spill over their white boundaries. She listened as Dad outlined the day's schedule.

"Once Jim and Joe have the cattle gathered, they will hold them in the back pasture. After the cows have paired up with their calves, we'll drive them to the river hills and make sure they get settled. Then we'll ride to the cabin and meet Mom there around supper time."

"Do you girls have all your bedding and clothes ready to go?" Mom asked.

"Mine's by the door," Brooke replied. Mom was going to haul the food, bedding, and clothes down to the river in the big 4x4 pickup. It was easier than using pack horses.

Brooke finished the last of her toast and jam and brushed the crumbs from her hands. She gathered up her plate, utensils, and cup and carried them to the sink. "Thanks for breakfast, Mom!"

"Don't worry about the dishes. I'll do them," Mom said.

Joining Skye at the entry, Brooke slid into her riding boots and denim coat. She pulled a cowboy hat onto her head. A hat protected her face and head from the prickles and pokes of tree branches she might encounter.

"Hey, don't forget your slicker," Skye reminded her.

"Right." Brooke grabbed her leather raincoat from the closet. The coat reached almost down to her boots and was waterproofed to repel rain. This time of year, it was unwise to go riding without it. Storms could appear without warning.

"Ready?" Skye asked as she stepped outside the door.

Brooke nodded. On the outside, she was ready as she could be. But on the inside, she had her doubts. If only she knew how Jazz would react to the cows. Dad said she came from a ranch, so that should mean Jazz would be used to the excitement that could sometimes erupt around animals. But after yesterday's runaway, she wasn't so sure.

Brooke reached down and took hold of her gear. "See ya, Mom!" she called out.

"One minute!" Mom came into the entry and slipped a couple of granola bars and two small bags of jerky into the front pocket of Brooke's coat. "Take these in case you get hungry on the ride. I doubt you'll have time to stop for lunch. Make sure to give the extra to Skye."

"Sure. Thanks." Brooke slipped outside and placed the gear inside the pickup. At the barn, she got Jazz ready and tied her slicker to the saddle. Remembering the broken rein, she went to the tack room to see if she could find one to replace it.

Dad entered the small room and took a coiled lariat off the wall. "What are you looking for?"

"My rein broke yesterday so I was trying to find another one." Brooke held up her bridle for Dad to see the ripped leather.

"How did you manage that?"

Brooke explained what happened. She hadn't told him about the runaway yesterday because he didn't approve of her and Skye racing their horses. She braced herself for stern words, but was met with chuckles instead. Surprised, she asked, "What's so funny?"

"The people we bought Jazz from told us she was like dynamite when she ran. They said one little kissing sound was all it took to get her fired up."

"But I didn't make a . . ." Brooke stopped. She hadn't made the sound, but Skye had. Jazz must have heard it and thought Brooke had cued her to run. Relief squeezed out the doubts that were lingering in her mind. She didn't have a crazy horse. Maybe this cattle drive would be fun after all.

Dad reached up to the selection of bridles that hung on the wall. "Use this one for Jazz. I will bring some extra leather and see if I can fix yours at the river."

Brooke bridled Jazz and rode out to the cattle with Dad and Skye. She watched Jazz closely for any signs of nervousness. Cows mooed loudly trying to find their calves. The nasal bellows of the calves calling to their moms was deafening. Through it all, Jazz held her head low, which was a good sign that the commotion wasn't bothering her. Brooke relaxed a little more and watched as the cows ran from calf to calf, sniffing them until they found their own.

"I never understood how one calf can smell different from another," Brooke said. "I'm glad Mom and Dad don't have to do that to identify us!"

Skye laughed. "That would be funny! I wonder how we would smell."

Dad looked at the girls and grinned. "You would smell like monkeys because you're full of bananas! You wait here while I go and see if we're ready to start."

Brooke was still giggling with Skye when Dad waved for them to come over.

"We'll be taking the cows through the gate that is north of the bluff of pine trees at the top of the river," Dad directed. "Most of these cows know where that is, so hopefully we won't have any troubles. Jim and Joe will watch the sides. Skye and Brooke, it will be your job to follow along at the back and make sure the cows and calves keep up. I'll ride wherever I'm needed."

Brooke nodded. She had helped in lots of cattle drives before with Buckshot, and was used to riding at the back. As long as Jazz knew what she was doing, everything should be fine.

"All right, let's move out!" Dad ordered.

Jim and Joe rode along on each side of the herd to get them started in the right direction. When they turned back into the field, Brooke watched Jim ride close to the front on the left side. This pushed the swirling mob back toward the direction of river. Once the lead cows figured out where they needed to go, Brooke and Skye chased the rest from the back.

"Hee-yah, cows! Let's go! Yep! Yep!" Brooke yelled at the herd of black before her. They swarmed toward the open gate, and soon the whole herd streamed out of the fence and ran down the road, leaving a cloud of dust behind them. The cattle drive was off to a spirited but smooth start.

To catch up to the cows, Brooke cued Jazz into a lope. The gentle back and forth movement reminded her of a rocking chair, even though she was on the back of a horse. Entering the billowing veil of grey dust, Brooke struggled to see. She slowed Jazz to a walk, not wanting to lose a wayward cow that might be lost in the cloud. After a few minutes, the dust began to settle as the cows slowed to a walk. She glanced behind her and was glad to see there were no stragglers.

Dad rode up beside her on Chocolate. "How is she doing?"

Brooke licked her lips to moisten her mouth before she answered and grimaced at the layer of dirt that was already covering her. "She's doing well. She doesn't mind the cows, and she's smooth to ride."

"Jazz is a good ranch horse, so this should be easy for her. In fact, she . . ." Dad's voice stopped as a group of four calves broke free from the herd and raced back to the pasture they had just left. Calves often did this when they changed grazing locations and lost their mothers in the confusion of the move. They wanted to return to where they had last seen their mothers.

Brooke tried to stop one of the calves. Jazz darted to the right but the calf scooted to the left and got away.

"Brooke!" Dad yelled. "Come on! We've got to get them stopped before they get away on us!"

CHAPTER

9

DAD WHIRLED CHOCOLATE AROUND AND LEFT Brooke behind in the dust. Brooke knew that he would try to get ahead of the calves to turn them. When this happened she would need to be in position behind Dad creating a moving wall. This would prevent the calves from ducking behind him.

Heart pounding, Brooke took a deep breath and moved her right foot to Jazz's shoulder. Jazz swiftly spun a semicircle on her back legs. Brooke grabbed the saddle horn to keep from being catapulted through the air. This horse was quick in more ways than one.

Jazz was eager to chase after the strays, but Brooke held her in. After yesterday's episode, she was hesitant to run. She cued Jazz into a lope, but knew it wouldn't be fast enough. Dad had already reached the calves. She hoped they would return to the herd, but her wish was short lived. While the two front calves turned back, the last two darted behind Chocolate and kept running.

"Brooke!" Dad commanded. "Get up here!"

Brooke's heart pounded. She wanted to help, but fear held her back. There was a battle going on within her, and right now panic was getting the upper hand. As she struggled with her decision, two blurs shot past her: Indee and Tuffy. Skye was going to do what Brooke couldn't. She jerked on her reins in frustration. Jazz's head flew up as she slid to a stop.

"Sorry, girl. It's not your fault."

She watched as Skye and Indee darted after the two strays, turning them back toward the herd, with Tuffy nipping at their heels. Dad was following the first two calves. Brooke couldn't meet his eyes when he stopped beside her.

"What on earth were you doing?" Dad growled.

Brooke shook her head. She didn't know what to say. How could she tell him that she was too afraid? He wouldn't understand. Nothing ever scared him.

The frown of disappointment that Dad gave her cut deeper than any words could. "Take these calves back to the herd. Then stay there and stop any others from getting away. I'll go help Skye get those other two back." He spun around and rode away.

Brooke chased the calves back to the herd, struggling to hold in her tears. She had messed up big time. It wasn't hard to see Dad wasn't happy with her. And, of course, Skye had rushed in to save the day. That was like putting salt on an open wound.

The calves rejoined the herd, bawling for their mothers. Brooke and Jazz took up their position at the back. In a few minutes the two calves Skye was chasing shot past Brooke and disappeared within the herd.

When Brooke saw Skye riding toward her, she turned Jazz away and walked to the other side of the herd. She wasn't in any mood for talking right now. Her sister was Miss Fearless and could do anything. Dad was Mr. Logical and seemed to have an answer to any problem. No doubt he thought that since Brooke had her own horse again, she should be able to ride just as she had with Buckshot. But that wasn't the case. Brooke was certain neither of them would understand the struggle she was going through right now.

For the next three hours, Brooke made sure to stay out of Dad and Skye's way. She kept busy by driving any stragglers back into the herd. It was slow, dusty work, but Brooke didn't mind. She needed time to think. She had to come to a decision. What was she going to be? A coward or a cowgirl? She loved this ranch, and she loved the work. She liked her horse. Jazz was proving to be a reliable mount. The runaway yesterday hadn't been Jazz's fault, and it had proven to Brooke that she could still do what needed to be done. She just had to act in spite of her fear. Today, her fear had kept her from helping Dad, and judging by the disappointed looks he kept sending her, she had let him down in a big way.

"We're almost there." Skye's voice broke into Brooke's thoughts.

Looking ahead, Brooke saw Dad ride out in front of the cattle. He opened the wire gate and leaned it up against the fence. The cows must have sensed they were getting close, for they picked up speed. Brooke couldn't help but smile at their eagerness. Huge cows with their ballooning sides barreled their way to the gate. Their frisky calves followed in pursuit, with their tails straight up in the air. Together they poured through the gate and ran down the hill.

"Come inside the fence," Dad ordered. "We will keep an eye on them for a while to make sure the calves stay put."

From inside the gate, Brooke watched as the cows and calves feasted on the green pasture. They would snatch some mouthfuls of grass and then walk ahead a few steps for another bite. In this way, they slowly spread out over the hillside. She saw two calves try to run off, but Joe turned them back. After the herd was settled, she saw Dad ride Chocolate toward the gate. She followed as the rest of the riders left the pasture.

Dad closed the gate and climbed into the saddle. He turned Chocolate to face Jim and Joe. "We'll see you guys in a week?"

"Yup! You shouldn't have anything out of the ordinary to look after. The fences are fixed, and the cattle are looking good." Jim paused. "Well, there is the river. You might want to keep an eye on it. The water level seems to be dropping."

As Brooke listened, she remembered that Dad had mentioned "disappearing water" when they had lost Jazz, and she had noticed how quiet the river was on their ride. In light of what Jim was saying, the pieces to a puzzle were beginning to fit together.

Dad nodded. "Yesterday Joe mentioned something about the lack of water in the river. I don't know what's happening, but as long as it keeps flowing, we should be all right. It's not as if it is going to vanish."

"That would be something. Vanishing rivers. What next?" Joe tipped his hat to say goodbye. "We'll see you guys around! With these two cowgirls to help you, maybe next year we can take a whole month off."

Dad glanced at Brooke before he replied. "Someday— maybe."

Brooke watched Dad in shock. Someday? Maybe? Hurt, she looked away. For as long as she could remember, she had wanted to work alongside Dad, helping him with the ranch work. Now it sounded like he thought that might not be possible.

"If we're going to make it to the cabin by supper time, we'd better get going. We have a lot of ground to cover." Dad turned Chocolate and left the gate.

Brooke pulled Jazz in behind Chocolate and Indee. As they followed the hilltop trail that wound its way through the grass and wildflowers, Brooke couldn't forget what Dad had said. A fierce determination filled her heart. By the end of the week, she was going to prove him wrong. She didn't know how, but she was going to show him that she had the courage to be a top-notch cowgirl.

Fear was no longer welcome.

CHAPTER

10

BROOKE LOOPED HER REINS OVER THE saddle horn and slid down to the ground. She stomped her feet in an attempt to loosen the damp pant legs that clung like glue. After three hours of riding, it was refreshing to stop in the grove of poplar trees. The canopy of leaves provided welcome relief from the suffocating heat of the afternoon sun. Lifting up her hat, she wiped the dampness from her forehead with the back of her hand. "If that sun had any more warmth, I would be well done."

Skye stepped down and removed her bridle from Indee. "Well done?" she questioned.

"As in sizzled, charbroiled, and scorched. I think my nose has burned to a crisp." Focusing both eyes downward, Brooke struggled to see the cherry-sized lump that jutted out from her face.

Skye snickered. "It looks like a clown nose, and when you cross your eyes like that, you could be one."

Brooke tilted her head to the side and stuck out her tongue at Skye, which only made her giggle harder. "And now whose face is red?" she chuckled. Skye rarely got a sunburn due to her dark complexion, but when she began to laugh, her face turned as red as a bowl full of apples. Turning back to Jazz, she removed the bridle so Jazz could join Indee and Chocolate in snatching a few bites from the grass that waved in the light breeze.

"Keep an eye on the horses," Dad instructed as he propped himself against a tree. "I'm going to try to get a little shut eye." He stretched out his legs and tugged his hat down so it covered his face.

Brooke flopped down on the grass beside Skye. "I don't know how he can sleep like that. A tree trunk for a pillow. How can that be comfortable?"

Skye looked upwards. "I would rather sleep on one of those."

Brooke leaned back and placed her hands behind her head. The blue sky was dotted with clouds of all shapes and sizes. "Those would be more comfy," she agreed, "although I wouldn't want to sleep on that one. It's so skinny, it would only take one wrong turn, and I would fall off my bed of fluff."

"And you wouldn't get much sleep on that bandicoot cloud. It's so tiny, the only way you could rest on it would be if you were like a flamingo and could sleep with one foot in the air."

Brooke raised an eyebrow. "A bandi-what cloud? You made that up."

"I did not," Skye protested. "I read about bandicoots a few nights ago. They live in Australia and look like gigantic mice or squirrels, only without the fluffy tail. Their noses are long and thin—like sharpened pencils. And they like to hop." Skye pointed. "See, there's one right there, behind your skinny bed."

Brooke followed Skye's finger with her eyes. "I think I see it, but he appears to be gliding more than hopping through the air."

"Hopping clouds! That would be funny to see."

Sharing a laugh with Skye, Brooke agreed, "That would be something: watching them play leapcloud instead of leapfrog." Their game continued for a while, but then, growing tired of cloud watching, Brooke rolled over onto her stomach. Resting her chin in her hands, she watched the horses graze. "I wonder why the grass doesn't tickle their noses when they eat."

Skye grabbed a handful of grass. "Does it tickle yours?"

"Hey!" Brooke hollered as the blades swished past her nose. Twisting her face away, she snatched some grass of her own and thrust it at Skye. Soon they were in an all-out grass war. Tuffy joined in the fun, barking and yipping as tufts of green flew through the air.

"All right, girls, it's time to make a mile," Dad's voice cut through the laughs, screeches, and barks.

Brooke eyed Dad, watching as he lifted his bridle off a tree branch and made his way over to Chocolate. Her eyebrows shot up as an idea darted into her mind. Glancing at Skye, she saw a mischievous look in her eyes. "Should we?" she whispered.

Skye grinned playfully. "Let's!"

Brooke snatched two handfuls of grass and waited as Skye did the same. She crouched down, and together they crept silently through the grass, like lions preparing to pounce on their prey.

"Cha-a-arge!" they yelled in unison. Dad whipped around, but he was too late. Brooke jumped up on his back. Hanging on with one arm around his neck, she stuffed grass down his checkered shirt. Skye came in and dove at his knees, tackling him to the ground.

It was a tangled jumble of boots, arms, hats, and grass. Dad finally held his arms up in defeat. "All right! All right! I surrender. You girls are too much for this old cowboy."

Brooke stood up and brushed the grass off her pants. "We could have told you that. You keep getting a little shorter every year."

"And a little slower," Skye added.

"Okay, you two. Let's see how quick you are. The last one in the saddle has to water the horses tonight." Dad's words spurred the girls into action.

Brooke bridled Jazz and stepped up into the saddle. She glanced over her shoulder in time to see Skye sit down at the same time. Who had won?

Dad rode up beside them. "I am impressed. You can move fast, and since it was a tie, both of you can water the horses tonight." Glancing at his watch he said, "If we want to make it to camp by supper, we'd better get moving."

Brooke took her place at the back of the line. A warm wind blew out of the valley as she broke over the top of the hill. She gazed into the serpentine channel the river had cut for itself over the years. Limestone cliffs shone like silver, and green meadows blazed with splashes of goldenrod wildflowers. Below them, large spruce trees rose like towering green giants swinging back and forth to the silent music of the wind. In those trees, hidden from sight, was the cabin where she would live for the next week—if she could get there. Brooke took a deep breath and tried to steady her nerves.

Ahead of her lay the treacherous trail where she had taken her last ride with Buckshot. The path wove back and forth across the hillside as it crossed the meadows and bypassed cliffs. In some places, it became so narrow that only one horse could walk on the trail at a time. One slip could send horse and rider plunging over the cliff into the depths of the valley below. With that thought, terrifying memories flooded into her mind, taking her back to that awful day.

Leaping off Buckshot, Brooke saw her worst nightmare come true. He fought valiantly to keep his footing on the slimy ground, but this was a battle he wouldn't win. Brooke watched in horror as he somersaulted over the limestone cliff.

"Buckshot, no!"

Frantically looking for a way to reach him, Brooke spotted a route down. The way was steep, so she leaned back and slid down the slippery slope.

"Is he okay?" Skye shouted down.

"I don't know yet. Just get Dad."

Brooke reached Buckshot and knelt beside him, looking for some indication that he was alive. Hope flared when he opened his eyes and looked at her. He lifted his head and nickered quietly. She rubbed his head and looked over the rest of his body to see if he had any injuries. Her hopes fizzled when she saw that two of his legs were twisted in places where they shouldn't be bent. Sobbing, she lifted his head into her lap and stroked his mane, knowing what would have to happen.

"Buckshot, I'm so sorry," she repeated again and again. When Dad arrived, he confirmed her fears. With two broken legs, their main concern was to end his suffering. Wincing at the thought, Brooke backed away and climbed up to the trail. Although Buckshot's pain would end, hers was just beginning.

Brooke's hand trembled as she wiped the tears from her eyes and cheeks. Fear clung to her like a pesky insect, urging her to pull back on the reins and turn around. But Brooke willed her hands to keep the reins slack. That fall had cost her so much: her horse, her courage, and her confidence. She would never again race the wind with Buckshot, but now she had Jazz. With her, she could gain back what she had lost. Despite the quivering in her legs and in her heart, she was determined to make a new start.

"Keep it steady girl," she whispered as she fixed her eyes on the black tips of Jazz's ears. She didn't look to the right or to the left until they reached the welcoming shade of the spruce trees in the bottom of the valley. When the horses stopped at the hitching rail, her cramped muscles began to relax. She slid out of the saddle and wrapped her arms around Jazz's neck. "Thank you," she exhaled with relief. She was surprised when Jazz rested her head on her shoulder, as if to say she understood.

Dad swung off Chocolate and removed his saddle. "When you have watered the horses, put them in the corral and fork them some hay. And since Mom is already here, once you have the chores done, you can put the gear into the cabin."

After she had removed Jazz's tack and put it away, Brooke led her and Chocolate to the river. The horses walked into the water and sank their noses into the ripples. Brooke sat down on a rock and listened to the peaceful song of the gurgling stream. As she examined her surroundings, she realized Dad was right. The water level was down.

"The river is low," Skye said, echoing Brooke's thoughts.

"Yeah, no wonder Dad's worried. I think the horses could walk across anywhere," Brooke stated. Usually they had to choose their crossings with care as there were locations where the only way to cross the river was to let the horses swim. "I hope it doesn't disappear."

"Disappear?" Skye snickered. "Rivers don't vanish."

Brooke laughed at the absurd idea. "No, I guess not. It's not like we'd wake up one morning and poof—the river would be gone." When the horses finished drinking, Brooke and Skye led them to the corral and forked them some hay from the round alfalfa bale that was outside the fence. With that done, they headed to the pickup to get the gear and supplies.

Slinging a backpack over her shoulder and taking two sleeping bags and pillows, Brooke walked to the old cabin. She could see Grandpa's and Dad's initials carved into the log by the door: "W.M." and "T.M."—for Wyatt and Todd Mackenzie. Like the barn, the cabin had been built by Grandpa many years ago, and not much had changed. Without electrical power or running water, and with an outhouse for a bathroom, Brooke always felt like she was stepping back in time when she came here.

Seeing that the door stood slightly ajar, Brooke poked her riding boot into the crack to open it the rest of the way. As she did, Tuffy ran up and let out a low growl. She watched as he crouched and snarled. What was he doing? Was something in there? Setting her gear on the ground, Brooke opened the door a little wider. Tuffy darted in.

Skye walked up beside her. "What's gotten into him?"

"I don't know. I barely opened the door and he rushed in."

"Why don't you look inside?"

Brooke shook her head. She wasn't going to stick her head in the door. What if it was something big in there? Something dangerous? It wouldn't be the first time a bear had found its way into the cabin, and judging by the fierceness of Tuffy's growl, whatever was in there wasn't good.

"Scared?" Skye teased.

"If you're so brave, why don't you go see what's inside?" Brooke snapped.

Brooke didn't have a chance to hear Skye's answer, for at that moment, the creature from inside the cabin scurried out and headed straight for her.

11

"EEEK!" BROOKE JUMPED TO THE SIDE as a small puff of gray fur with a bushy tail streaked over her boots toward a tree. Tuffy flew out of the cabin in hot pursuit. With a mighty leap, he pounced, but his prey clawed its way to safety in the branches of an evergreen.

Skye stared up at the tree. "What was that?"

Listening to the angry chatter being hailed down on Tuffy, Brooke answered, "That sounds like one angry squirrel." She laughed as Tuffy circled the base of the tree and then tried to jump up its side. "Lucky for him, Tuffy doesn't know how to climb."

Dad jogged over. "What's all the excitement about?"

Skye gave Brooke a cheeky smile and said, "Oh nothing, Brooke found a bandicoot in the cabin."

Dad's eyebrows shot up under the brim of his black hat. "A what?"

The clueless look on Dad's face made Brooke chuckle. For once she wasn't the one staring stupidly in confusion at Skye's strange bits of information.

"A bandicoot," Skye repeated.

Dad looked up at the tree where the squirrel continued to chatter his annoyance. He shrugged his shoulders, and said, "Well, squirrel or bandicoff, or whatever you call it, make sure you sweep out the cabin before putting all our stuff in there. Since Jim and Joe left here only yesterday, let's hope our furry resident didn't have the opportunity to make a big mess."

"Hey, you want to sweep? I'll go get the rest of the supplies out of the truck." Skye turned and ran to the pickup, leaving Brooke with no opportunity to answer.

"Looks like I'm sweeping then," Brooke muttered to herself. She took the well-aged bristle broom that was leaning against the cabin, and ducked inside. The doorway was low enough that, even at her height of five feet and five inches, she had to be careful not to scrape the top of her head on the door frame.

The shaded rays of the sun peeked through the one window of the cabin, giving Brooke enough light to see. The cabin wasn't large, but it was cozy. She swept around the wood stove and the small table and chairs that were to the left side of the door and then proceeded to one of the sets of bunk beds that were along the back wall. Moving on to the last set of stacked beds that stood opposite the table and chairs, Brooke found a crumpled black sock. Thinking it belonged to one of the ranch hands, she pushed it back under the bed. Hopefully they would find it when they returned after their vacation, as they stayed at the cabin during the summer months to be closer to the cattle.

A thin dust cloud swirled around her as she guided the dirt to the entrance. The door creaked as she pushed it open with her foot and flung the dirt outside one sweep at a time.

"Brooke!" Skye shouted and then coughed.

Brooke glanced up as she let another swoop of dust fly. What was bothering Skye now? Seeing the look of disgust on Skye's face as another shower of dust blew past her, it wasn't hard to guess. Brooke giggled.

"It's not funny," Skye snapped. "Now I have squirrel junk on me."

Brooke turned her back to hide her laughter. This would be the perfect chance to play a joke on Skye.

"You wouldn't believe the mess I found in here. I even found a large wrinkled black thing under one of the beds."

Skye's face went pale. She dropped her gear and feverishly brushed off her clothes.

Brooke kept a straight face, but it didn't last long. Taking pity, she said, "Don't worry about it, Skye. All I found was dust and an old black sock. The squirrel was not in here long enough to make a mess."

Skye paused her frantic movements and eyed Brooke cautiously. "Really?"

"Really." Brooke slipped outside and set the broom against the cabin wall. Smelling smoke from a fire, she encouraged, "C'mon. Let's get this stuff inside. I'm getting hungry." She slung a backpack over her shoulder and stuffed the pillows under her arm. Clutching two sleeping bags in her hands, she ducked through the door and turned to the bunk beds on the right hand side.

Skye clambered in behind Brooke with two duffle bags in tow. "I get the top bunk."

"No problem," Brooke agreed. She loathed sleeping on the top because she felt like she was lying in a coffin whenever she slept up there. Since the roof sloped downwards from the center of the cabin to the outer walls, there was only about two feet of head space on the side of the bed that was against the wall. At least on the bottom bunk there was room to sit up without bumping her head. After placing Skye's gear on her bed, Brooke unrolled her sleeping bag and put her pillow in place. She stuffed the bag with her clothes at the end of her bed and then put away the rest of the food and supplies. Once everything was in its place, she and Skye walked over to the campfire. Hamburgers sizzled on the grill that balanced on the rocks outlining the fire pit.

Dad sent a burger spinning in the air. He caught it on the flipper and placed it back on the grill. "You girls get it all put away?"

Brooke flopped down onto one of the wooden stump chairs that surrounded the fire pit. "Yup," she replied. Her stomach growled as she watched the smoke lazily float its way toward the treetops. When she was younger, she used to pretend she could float upwards on that smoke until she reached the sky, where she would hop on a cloud to travel to distant lands. When another rumble echoed inside her, she asked, "When will the burgers be done?"

"In about five minutes."

Five minutes would give her enough time to visit the red building that was hidden from view in the underbrush of the spruce trees. She stood up.

"Where are you going?" Skye asked.

"If you must know, I'm going to the outhouse," Brooke replied sarcastically.

"You'll have to beat me if you want to use it first!" Skye taunted and sprinted into the bush.

Brooke shook her head in annoyance at Skye and her racing. Sometimes it seemed like that was the only thing that occupied her mind.

"Hey, Brooke. Could you let Mom know that the burgers are almost ready?" Dad requested.

"Sure." She might as well do something while she was waiting for Skye. Walking to the pickup, she found Mom reaching inside to retrieve something.

"Here, take these." Mom handed Brooke a pan covered in tinfoil. "Careful, it's warm."

The sweet scent of cinnamon and sugar floated through the air and tingled her nose. Mmm. Her favorite. Fresh cinnamon buns. She placed the warm dish on the table. "Mom, Dad wanted me to . . ."

"Ahhh! Help!" A frantic cry split the air.

CHAPTER 12

"BEAR! THERE'S A BEAR!"

Brooke turned as Skye came charging out of the trees. Her eyes were like two round white plates with brown marbles in the center.

"I came out of the outhouse and saw a black shadow in the trees," Skye huffed. "It was the biggest bear I've ever seen. It was gigantic. It was this tall." She raised her hand up to her shoulder.

Dad got his rifle out of the pickup. "Where did you see the bear?"

Skye pointed. "On the other side of the outhouse."

Brooke watched as Dad made his way into the trees, followed closely by Tuffy. Expecting to hear the loud crack of the rifle, she was surprised when she heard, "Hee-yah! Hee-yah!" Brooke raised one eyebrow as she looked at Skye. Since when did Dad try to chase a bear away by yelling at it? Usually he would shoot into the air to scare it off.

Tuffy barked, and soon a black shadow lumbered out of the trees, coming straight toward them.

"See, it's huge. Quick run to the cabin," Skye cried out as she turned to run.

Brooke took a closer look at the shadow and then laughed.

"Skye, come back. It's not a bear, silly. It's a black cow."

"A cow?"

"Yeah, a really scary one," Brooke kidded.

Skye's face turned red. She opened her mouth and then snapped it shut.

Brooke enjoyed a good chuckle. Skye was rarely speechless.

The cow charged past them and ran toward the river. Tuffy was hot on her heels, and a small black calf with a white face followed behind, bawling as he tried to keep up. In a few moments Dad came out of the bush.

"Did you see your bear?"

Skye's mouth turned down. "Yes," she mumbled.

"I am glad you saw the cow as I found wolf tracks in the bushes close to where she was. We haven't had wolf trouble this year, but if they are in the neighborhood, we will have to keep our eyes open."

The evening soon passed, and Brooke said goodnight to Dad and Mom. She was tired and wanted to get some sleep. As she went into the cabin, she heard the truck rumble to life and then leave, as Mom returned to the ranch house.

Dad poked his head into the cabin. "Wake-up will be at five-thirty. We have to get a good start in the morning."

"Okay," Brooke answered, glad she had decided to go to bed early. She slipped into tomorrow's clothes and climbed into bed. She didn't sleep fully dressed at home, but the cabin was different. She hated putting on cold clothes in the morning, so she always went to bed dressed. Skye gave her a hard time, but that didn't stop Brooke. It was worth having warm clothes in the morning when the air was chilly.

Brooke awakened to the thwack of an ax striking a piece of wood. She could smell bacon in the air. She rolled onto her back and opened her eyes. The morning light streamed in the window. Glancing at her watch, she saw it was five-thirty. She sat up in bed and ran her fingers through her hair, wrinkling her nose at the scent of smoke that clung to it. While she wasn't fond of the aroma, it was a natural insect repellant. She gathered her hair and pulled it up into a ponytail once again with the fluorescent pink elastic. Lifting her sock feet over the edge of the bed, Brooke slipped them into her riding boots. Another advantage of being already dressed was that it didn't take long to get ready in the morning.

Brooke stood up and shook Skye's sleeping bag. "Hey, you. Better get up. Dad's already got the food going. I'm going to wash up." She poked at the sleeping bag again, this time a little harder.

"Okay, okay."

Brooke shook her head at the grouchy, muffled reply that came from the depths of the sleeping bag. How could Skye sleep under the covers like that? Even when it was cold, Brooke still had to have a little peephole to let fresh air in. Otherwise, she felt like she was suffocating. Snatching her towel from the end of her bed, she opened the door to the cabin. The hinges creaked, showing their age.

Brooke stepped outside and took a deep breath. She enjoyed early mornings in the outdoors. The aroma of the trees, the river, and the dirt blended to create a fresh perfume that could not be bought in a store. This morning, the air was sweetened with the faint scent of cinnamon. Brooke hurried down to the river to wash up, knowing Dad must have put the leftover cinnamon buns on the fire to warm.

She inhaled sharply as the icy freshness of the water splashed away the last remnants of sleep. Water droplets slid down her cheeks and landed back in the gurgling river. As she dried her face on the soft towel, she could hear the chatter of the squirrel or "Boots"—short for Bandicoot—as Skye had named him last night.

"Breakfast is ready." Dad's voice silenced Boots' tirade for a few seconds, but it wasn't long before the air was filled with his persistent prattle once again. As she ran to the cabin to put her towel away, Brooke hoped this wouldn't be a regular occurrence every morning. It wasn't very peaceful.

Reaching the cabin, she pulled open the door and ducked her head to go inside. "Ouch," Brooke exclaimed as sharp pain instantly exploded in her head. Rubbing the top of her skull, she stepped back. Skye tumbled out the door in front of her. "Sorry about that. I didn't see you."

Skye grimaced as she held her forehead. "Obviously," she said dryly. "At least I'm awake now."

Although she knew the cabin was empty, Brooke entered slowly and tossed the towel on her bed; then walked back out to where the food sat waiting on an old wooden table beside the fire. The smell of cinnamon buns made her mouth water. Taking a fork, she speared one and dropped it onto a scratched, tin plate. She added two slices of bacon and joined Dad and Skye around the fire. It would have been quiet and peaceful, except for Boots' continual exercise of his vocal chords.

"Boots, be quiet," Brooke ordered before biting into the gooey syrup that dripped from the cinnamon bun.

"Boots?" Dad questioned. "Who's that?"

Brooke licked off her fingers and then pointed to the tree where the gray fur ball watched them with his glassy black eyes. "That's him right there. The squirrel. Skye named him Boots because he's a bandicoot wannabe."

"Mm-hmm." Dad shook his head and smiled. "When you girls are done eating, wash up the dishes and get the lunches ready. Don't forget your water bottles. We have a long way to go today. I'll go catch the horses." He filled his coffee mug one more time before heading to the corral.

"Do you want to wash the dishes, and I'll get the food?" Skye asked.

"Sounds like a plan," Brooke agreed. She didn't mind doing dishes. The warm water helped to keep the early-morning chill at bay. She stacked the dirty dishes on the picnic table and then retrieved an old metal washtub from the cabin. She got warm water from the cooker, which was a large pot that had a fire underneath to heat the water. Steam rose from the old metal dish as she poured in the warm liquid. Adding a squirt of soap, she swished the water until white bubbles appeared.

After washing the dishes and putting them away, Brooke picked up two five-gallon pails and carried them over to the old pump. As she moved the handle up and down, clear water gushed out the spout and splashed into the pails. After they were full, she carried the water to the cooker and poured it in. Skye was waiting with the saddle packs. They grabbed their riding gloves and water bottles and went to the tack shed where Dad had finished brushing the horses.

Once saddled, they rode out of camp and up the hillside. The fog hung low in the valley, and as they climbed through the mist, Brooke could almost imagine that they were riding on a cloud. But, as the sun rose higher in the sky, the fog slowly disappeared until it vanished completely.

"Which pasture are we going to, Dad?" Brooke asked when they stopped to let their horses catch their breath. She knew the cattle were split up into five groups of two hundred animals each and then placed in different pastures for the summer. They would try to get to each herd this week to make certain the cattle were healthy.

Dad pointed downriver to the east. "We're riding out to the farthest fence today. Joe and Jim said that they haven't been there in over a week. We'll need to keep up a good pace to ensure we can spend enough time to get a good check on them."

He looked at Jazz and said, "This will be a good test to see how your horse does in the tough terrain."

Brooke rubbed Jazz's neck. Her confidence in her little horse was growing. So far, she had handled the trail like a pro. "She's sure-footed and doesn't need to be encouraged to keep in step with the other horses."

Skye looked down at her. "She even keeps up to Indee."

Brooke nodded. At 16.2 hands or about five and a half feet at his withers, the place where his mane ended on his back, Indee was one of the tallest horses on the ranch. With his long legs, he could cover ground quickly. Most horses had to trot to keep up with him. Brooke had always thought that was why he was Skye's favorite.

"I'm hoping to be at the pasture by eleven o'clock, so we'd better get going." Dad led the way into a small grove of trees ahead of them.

Brooke rolled up the sleeve of her coat and looked at her watch. It was seven. She followed Indee into the trees and settled in for a long ride.

Over four hours later, they reached their destination. "We made it," Dad said. "And there's our first herd to check." He motioned with his head to a group of cattle that were grazing on the hill below them. "We'll stop here and have a bite to eat. Unbridle your horses and let them grab a few nibbles too."

After unbridling Jazz, Brooke joined Dad and Skye on a grassy knoll and watched the calves play. While the mothers were busy eating, the calves kept themselves entertained by playing tag and follow the leader. When they got too far away, a mother would let out a thunderous bellow that echoed across the limestone cliffs. The calves would stop, turn around, and run back. Brooke smiled as she chewed on a piece of granola bar. They ran for the joy of running. It wasn't a contest to see who was the fastest.

Tossing a piece of jerky to Tuffy, Dad pointed to the frolicking calves. "See that black calf over there?"

"Which one, Dad?" Skye questioned. "There are about fifty down there."

"The one right near the front. I think he's limping on one of his hind legs. Let's watch a bit more to make certain he is. Skye, remember you have the medicine with you on Indee. You'll have to come and help me treat the calf."

Brooke tried not to let her disappointment show. Carrying the medication bags had always been her job when she had Buckshot. She suspected Dad had put them on Indee because he trusted Skye to be able to help him.

Watching the calf a few more minutes confirmed Dad's suspicions. It definitely had a sore foot. Brooke could see it limping on its back left leg. They finished eating, got on their horses, and rode down to the cows. Dad took out his lariat. Uncoiling enough rope to make a loop, he flipped the rope back and forth over his arm to get the twist out. He did a couple of practice twirls over his head. Brooke could feel her excitement growing. She loved to watch Dad rope. He had taught her to rope while standing on the ground, and she seemed to have a natural talent for it. While she had never roped from a horse, she hoped to try one day.

Dad leaned forward in the saddle. "All right, Chocolate, let's do it."

Chocolate didn't need any encouragement to go. He surged ahead and closed in on the group of calves. As they zeroed in on the injured one, the rest of the calves peeled away until all that were left was Dad, Chocolate, and the calf.

Chocolate pulled in close behind his target, his hooves beating the ground like a drum. Dad swung his lariat and let it fly. The rope floated through the air and landed neatly over the head of the calf. While Chocolate slid to a stop, Dad dallied the rope, wrapping it around the saddle horn to keep the calf from escaping and running off with the rope. Jumping out of the saddle, Dad kept one hand on the rope as he ran to the calf and tipped it onto the ground. He tied up three of its legs while Chocolate stood like a rock.

As Brooke rode with Skye to bring Dad the medications, the calf let out a nasal, ear-piercing bawl. A short distance away a black cow raised her head and looked toward her calf. Realizing it was her little one calling out in distress, she let out a powerful *Moooo* and charged straight toward Dad and the calf.

CHAPTER 13

THE ANGRY COW STORMED ACROSS THE pasture, her short legs pounding the ground, her bulges swaying from side to side. A shot of dread darted through Brooke. If the cow wasn't stopped before she reached Dad, she might plow right over him.

Skye kicked Indee into action. "C'mon, Brooke. We've got to stop her."

Brooke could feel every fiber of her being straining to go with Skye, except for that cord of fear that bound her with its iron grip. It was like the springtime mud that suctioned her boots to the ground so she couldn't move. She remembered being told that the only power fear could have was the control she gave it. If that was so, why was it so hard to break free of it? She didn't try to give fear control, it just seemed to take charge on its own. Desire and fear battled within her as she watched the scene play out before her.

Skye raced ahead but the cow reached the target first. Dad scrambled to the other side of the calf, placing it between him and the mad mother. The snorting brute slid to a halt, sniffed her calf, and then shoved her black nose a few inches from Dad's face. She let out an angry bellow and then shook her head threateningly.

Skye and Indee slid into place and were able to move the cow back a few feet, but their success was short-lived. The cow went around the other side and returned to the calf. Brooke could see the cow was annoyed. She lowered her head and kicked up dust in the air as she pawed the ground with her hoof. That was enough to spur Brooke into action. She felt the grip of fear break when she saw the danger Dad was in. She had heard too many tales about cowboys who had been mauled by a cow. She didn't want Dad to become one of those stories.

"Let's go! They need our help." Brooke squeezed Jazz's sides with her legs and they bolted toward the cow. Once they arrived, they worked with Skye to move the cow back about twenty feet. Brooke relaxed a little. With two horses they would be able to keep the cow away while Dad treated the calf.

"Skye, get the medications here quick," Dad yelled. "Brooke, stay on your horse and keep her between us and the cow. The cow didn't charge over me, so I think she's trying to bluff us. I don't think she'll do anything, but I don't want to take any chances."

Brooke didn't dare take her eyes off the cow as Skye turned Indee around and left. She had forgotten that Skye had the medications. Her heart raced. How was she was supposed to protect Dad and Skye by herself? What would happen if the cow got past her? Skye hadn't been able to keep the cow away on her own, and she was fearless. Brooke took a deep breath. She might be scared, but Dad was counting on her.

"All right, Jazz," Brooke murmured. "It's up to us. We've got to keep that cow away from them. If we don't, they'll get hurt." Brooke saw Jazz's ears flick back and then forward again. She hoped Jazz understood what they had to do. As the cow started toward them, Brooke felt Jazz's muscles tense beneath the saddle and she exploded into action.

Jazz leaped to the left as the cow tried to duck around them. The cow scooted to the other side. Brooke clutched the saddle horn as Jazz spun hard to the right, slamming the door shut to the opening the cow was trying to force her way through. The cow darted to the left, then right, and left again. Brooke gripped the saddle tightly with her legs as Jazz sprang back and forth, matching the cow move for move. The cow sprinted hard to the right. Jazz launched herself forward and in two strides stopped the cow. The cow changed direction. Jazz turned with her and stopped the cow in her tracks. The cow let out a frustrated moo, but didn't try to get around Jazz again.

Brooke's breath came in quick bursts as she reached down and rubbed Jazz's sweaty neck. Wow! What a ride. What a horse. It had taken all of her strength to cling to the saddle so she didn't fly off as Jazz cut back and forth. Even Buckshot hadn't been able to work a cow like that.

"Brooke, we're done."

Even though she heard Dad's words, Brooke didn't take her eyes off the cow until she saw the calf run past to its mom. They sniffed noses and trotted away. Now that she had her baby back, the cow no longer saw them as a threat. Brooke patted Jazz's neck one more time and then turned around. Dad coiled up his rope while Skye placed the medications back in the bag.

"Good job, Brooke. You handled that like a pro."

Brooke couldn't stop her smile. Finally. She had done something right, and Dad had noticed. "Jazz knew what needed to be done. I only pointed her at the cow, and she took over, matching the cow move for move."

"Jazz is a ranch horse. She has been used for sorting cows, chasing cows, and has had many miles of checking cows. In fact, she is also a trained rope horse. That is one of the reasons we bought her for you." Dad smiled up at her. "You can already rope from the ground. Now it's time to try from the saddle."

Brooke could hardly contain her excitement. She slid to the ground and gave Dad a huge hug. Her own rope horse? She couldn't believe it. Over Dad's shoulder she caught sight of Skye and was surprised to see a scowl on her face. What was up with that?

"Take this lariat," Dad said as he gave it to her. "I brought an extra one along so you could get some practice swinging a rope from the saddle."

A shiver charged through Brooke's fingertips as they closed around the rope. To be able to rope from a horse was a dream come true. She climbed into the saddle and uncoiled the rope until she had a loop that hung from her shoulder to her knee.

She twirled it over her head a couple of times. Jazz stood quietly and didn't flinch when the rope touched her side as Brooke stopped twirling.

Dad pointed to a tree stump that jutted out of the grass like a giant toothpick. "Practice throwing it over that stump. Skye and I will finish checking the rest of the cattle on this flat and then come back and see how you are doing."

Anticipation coursed through Brooke as she nodded in reply. She smiled at Dad and was surprised when she saw the sour look on Skye's face. What was her problem? She tried to share a smile with her, but Skye spun Indee around and rode away. Brooke shook her head. Sisters.

Once she had Jazz lined up with the stump, Brooke lifted her rope and focused on the target. Twirling the loop over her head three times, she let it fly. It sailed through the air, past the stump, and landed in the grass on the other side. Although her aim had been good, she had overthrown. She coiled the rope back in, set her loop, and threw again. This time, the distance was right, but the rope landed to the left of the stump. Brooke pulled the rope in again, determined to get it right. Shaking the loop so that it hung freely, she twirled once more and let it fly.

"Bullseye!" she exclaimed as the rope settled over the target. She tried to flip the rope off the stump, but it was stuck. She cued Jazz to walk forward until she was able to shake the rope free. Looking over her shoulder she saw that Dad and Skye were still busy with the cows. Pulling on the reins so that Jazz backed up into place, she said, "Looks like there is time for a few more throws." She repeatedly tossed the rope and focused all her concentration on learning how to do it right.

"Good throw," Dad said. "Looks like you're getting the hang of it."

Brooke jumped and almost dropped the rope. She hadn't even heard them ride up. Thankfully, that had been a successful throw. She had missed the previous three.

"You only forgot one thing. You have to remember to dally." Dad demonstrated how to wrap the rope around the saddle horn two or three times. "If you would have caught a calf with that toss, you would have lost your rope, and right now we would be having fun trying to get it back." Dad gave her a grin. "Always keep in mind to throw and then dally."

"Throw and dally," Brooke whispered under her breath. Just when she got the hang of one thing, she had to remember something else.

"Try it," Dad encouraged. "Like this." He threw his rope and as soon as it went over the stump he made two loops around the saddle horn. "Make at least two circles, and be sure to keep your fingers free of the loops. It really hurts when they get pinched."

Brooke took a deep breath. The pressure was on. She circled the rope over her head three times and prepared to let it go.

"Look out!" Skye yelled. "There's a bee."

Startled, Brooke jerked her arm as the rope left her fingertips, causing the rope to veer off course and land ten feet from the stump. Brooke scanned the area. There was no bee. Seeing a smug smile on Skye's face, anger welled up in Brooke. "Skye, you ruined my throw."

Skye protested. "There was a bee."

"Where?" Brooke seethed. Although she didn't know for certain that there had not been a bee, she did know that Skye was pleased she had missed her toss.

"Hey, calm down. It's all right. Try again," Dad said.

Calm down? Try again? Not only had Skye messed up her throw, now Dad thought she was losing control. Gritting her teeth, Brooke coiled the rope until the loop sat in her right hand.

"Okay, one more time. You can do it."

Squishing down her frustration, Brooke focused on making this a successful throw.

"You got it. Dally! Dally! Dally!"

Brooke followed Dad's instructions and looped the rope around the horn of her saddle.

"Good job. Get into the habit of always doing that when you throw, and before you know it, you'll be a pro."

Brooke managed a smile. Dad's praise was encouraging. As they continued to check the cows, she kept throwing her rope at objects that they walked past. She caught a rock, a shrub, and a branch, and each time she practiced securing the rope to the saddle horn. With each toss she could feel her confidence growing.

After finding and checking the rest of the scattered cows, Dad said, "Well, that's it. Let's go home. It's been a long day." He turned Chocolate upriver toward the cabin. Skye followed, and Brooke brought up the rear. Even though they were miles away, Jazz seemed to understand that they were heading back. Her ears perked up, and her steps were light.

As they came to a river crossing, Brooke decided to throw the rope one more time. Why not try to catch her sister?

Skye and Indee had reached the middle of the river when Brooke let her loop fly. She watched as it sailed neatly over Skye's head and fell to her waist. Without thinking Brooke did as she had practiced.

She dallied.

CHAPTER 14

"AHHH!" SKYE'S HIGH-PITCHED SCREAM CHASED ITSELF across the valley to the other side of the river, along with Indee.

Brooke eyes' widened in surprise as the rope stretching from her saddle to Skye tightened and yanked Skye out of her saddle. For one distressing moment she watched as Skye hung suspended in the air before she yielded to gravity's pull. Drops of water exploded upwards from the river as Skye sank beneath its surface. Brooke winced. When she had decided to rope Skye, this had not been part of the plan.

A second later, Skye resurfaced. Frantically, Brooke released the rope from the saddle horn as she slid to the ground. Skye's arms were pinned to her sides by the rope, and she seemed unable to find her balance. She swayed back and forth like a tree in a wind storm.

"Hang on, Skye. I'm coming." Brooke gripped the end of the rope in her right hand and dashed into the river. Water spattered onto her shirt and jeans as she fought against the flow of the current. The water felt cool as it crept above her knees and continued to climb halfway up her legs. Brooke stretched out her hands to catch Skye as she toppled forward, but she wasn't close enough. Skye sank beneath the murky water a second time. Brooke plunged her hands under the water to pull Skye up.

"Brooke!" Skye sputtered as she resurfaced. "What were you trying to do? Drown me?"

Brooke was silent as she took in Skye's livid face beneath the strands of hair that clung to her like a spider's web. A storm was brewing inside her sister. She looked ready to burst, and Brooke knew she couldn't blame her.

"I'm sorry, Skye. I didn't mean to pull you into the water." Brooke apologized meekly as she loosened the rope from Skye's waist and lifted it over her head.

"Oh, and I suppose your rope just accidentally found its way over my head?" Skye fumed sarcastically.

Brooke didn't respond as Skye turned her back and waded to the bank where Indee stood eating grass. When Skye was this angry it was best to remain quiet and give her time to cool down. Hanging onto the rope to keep it from being carried away by the river's flow, Brooke sloshed her way across. Sitting down beside Skye on the bank, Brooke began to coil up her dripping rope and waited, knowing Skye would speak when she was ready.

Skye dumped the water out of her boots. "So, tell me again, what were you trying to do?"

Brooke peeked at Skye, trying to gauge the level of her temper. Her face was no longer fiery red, and some of the fury had left her voice. Taking that as a good sign, Brooke explained, "When you shouted about seeing that bee, you messed up my throw, and I wanted to prove to you that I could rope. Catching you seemed like a good way to do that, but I didn't plan on pulling you into the river. I was as stunned as you were when you fell off Indee's back."

Brooke waited for Skye to erupt, but she didn't. Instead, she picked up a rock and tossed it into the river. It landed with a plop, and its ripples fanned out in greater circles until they were overpowered and carried away by the current.

"I did see a bee, but I didn't have to yell as loud as I did," Skye confessed as she threw another rock. "I didn't want you to make that throw, because—well, you can rope and I can't."

Brooke's eyebrows shot up in amazement. She hadn't expected Skye to admit that, but now she could understand why Skye had tried to make her miss that throw. She had been jealous—an emotion Brooke often felt when Skye continually beat her in a foot race. Brooke finished coiling her rope. Maybe in the future she would try to be more understanding and congratulate Skye after a win instead of fuming with envy.

Skye flung another rock into the river and then pointed. "How are you going to get Jazz to this side? Do you think you could rope her and pull her over?"

Looking across to the opposite bank, Brooke estimated that the distance between her and Jazz was about a hundred feet. She dropped the coiled rope to the ground and stood up.

"That would be a good idea, but it's too far for my rope. I will have to go and get her." She grimaced as her boots gurgled with each step she took to the rivers' edge. She hated wet boots.

"What happened? Why is Jazz on the other side of the river? Brooke, did she buck you off?"

Brooke turned in time to see Dad emerge from the trees. Taking in a shaky breath, she nervously explained what had occurred while watching his face for any sign of anger. What would he say now?

Dad laughed out loud. "That's quite a story. It sounds like you're getting pretty good with your lariat, but you should save your roping skills for calves instead of your sister. We'll let you try it on another day. Right now, we need to get back to camp."

Brooke could hardly believe what Dad was saying. Rope calves? Excitement coursed through her as she stepped into the creek to go and get Jazz.

"Whoa! Where are you going?"

Brooke halted. "I have to get Jazz."

"Yes, I suppose you do. She isn't going to do you much good over there." Dad looked at her with a grin. "Why don't you try whistling first?"

"Whistle?"

"Yes, and be sure you make it loud enough for Jazz to hear you."

Puzzled, Brooke looked at Dad. His eyes twinkled back at her. He was clearly enjoying her confusion. Brooke put her fingers to her mouth and let out one shrill, clear whistle. Jazz's head came up and her ears perked forward.

"Whistle again," Dad directed.

She did and this time Jazz splashed across the river and came to a stop in front of her. "Do you have any other tricks under your mane that I don't know about?" Brooke whispered in amazement as she rubbed Jazz's head. Her horse continually surprised her. Coming in response to a whistle was quite clever. No other horse on the ranch did that. Seeing that Skye and Dad were mounting up, Brooke picked up her rope and tied it to the saddle. She put her left foot into the stirrup and pulled herself onto Jazz's back.

Guiding Jazz onto the trail behind Chocolate and Indee, Brooke hoped they'd make it to camp quickly. Her jeans felt like pieces of cold, wet cardboard stuck to her legs. It was a clammy feeling, and despite the warmth of the early evening air, a chill was creeping into her bones. She was relieved when camp came into sight.

With the horses put away, she slipped into the cabin, changed out of her wet clothes and hung them up to dry. Once supper was finished, she joined Dad and Skye by the fire. Pulling her knees up to her chest, she sipped her cup of hot chocolate and listened to the wood in the fire crackle and pop. Every so often a small explosion would shoot out a flurry of sparks that danced upwards into the darkening sky.

Sitting there in the darkness, Brooke could almost imagine that time stood still. Not a lot had changed in the ninety years since her great-grandpa's dad had come to homestead this land

and valley. She could remember the tales that Poppy, as she called her great-grandpa, had told them about growing up in a wild, untamed land and building the ranch up from nothing. He had passed on a little more than three years ago, and she missed listening to him. Looking across the flickering flames to Dad, she said, "Could you tell us a story about when Great-Grandpa was young?"

Dad pulled off his hat and tossed it onto a nearby stump. Leaning forward, he put his elbows onto his knees. His face glowed orange as he looked into the fire. "You know, this night reminds me of the first time Poppy told me about Old Pete." He pointed to the moon that hung like a huge flashlight in the sky. "The moon was almost full, just like it is tonight."

Brooke sat up a bit straighter. She had not heard about Old Pete before. "Who was he?"

"Old Pete's real name was Peter McGuire, and he was one of the first people to come to these here hills."

Brooke smiled as Dad's voice changed ever so slightly. She could almost see her white-haired Poppy sitting at the fire telling the story.

"No one knows how long he had been here, but he was pretty old when your Poppy was born."

"What did he do?" Skye asked.

"Old Pete was a miner. He was sure there was gold in these hills, and so he spent a lot of time looking for it in the spring and summer. He would find a small amount, but not enough to live on, so in fall and winter he'd come and work for Poppy's dad on the ranch. They became pretty good friends over the years."

Dad continued. "Old Pete was always helping people. He'd supply neighbors with loads of wood for winter heat or go hunting to supply meat for those that may be low on food. In return, people gave him a shirt, a coat, or a fresh meal. Back then, neighbors had to rely on each other. They looked out for one another. They were more than just people you lived beside. They were friends, and I think that's why everybody missed him so much when he disappeared."

Brooke shivered despite the warmth from the fire. "What happened?"

"No one really knows. It happened in the fall that Poppy turned eight. Old Pete stopped by the ranch. He was excited because he had found a rich vein of gold. He was eager to transport the gold he had mined into the bank for safekeeping. Poppy's dad told Old Pete that he had a trip to town planned for the following week. Pete promised to return at that time, but that week came and went, and he didn't show up. So Poppy's dad and a couple of neighbors went to Pete's cabin, which was located not too far from here."

"Did they find Pete?" Skye whispered.

Dad shook his head. "No. They found two small bags of gold in the cabin, but there was no trace of Pete or of his mining axe that he always carried with him. They thought something must have happened to him at his mine."

Brooke wrapped her arms around herself. This story was getting creepy. "Didn't they go to the mine and look for him?"

"They tried to, but no one knew where it was. He had kept it a well-guarded secret. All that was known was that it was located in one of the limestone caves in these hills. Since there are so many of them, it was impossible to check them all. They searched the ones around the cabin, but when they didn't find anything, they gave up looking."

"So he disappeared?" Brooke trembled. That was an eerie thought.

Dad nodded. "It sure seemed like he did, but a few nights later old Widow Simmons said she heard the distant sounds of something banging against a rock and a muffled cry for help."

"Was it Pete?" Skye asked.

"Poppy's dad thought it might be. He asked Widow Simmons where she had heard the noise, and she said that it seemed to be coming from under the ground."

"Under the ground?" Brooke shivered as a chill ran down her spine. She could almost feel her hair standing on end. This story was getting spooky.

"Under the ground," Dad repeated. "Poppy's dad got a neighbor to help him search the farm and spent one night out there under stars hoping to hear what Widow Simmons had heard. But in the end, they didn't find any trace of Old Pete."

Brooke watched as the glowing embers of the fire floated upwards until they disappeared from sight. That was what had happened to Old Pete. He had vanished into thin air.

"Poppy never forgot that story, and the summer he turned sixteen he decided to explore. The Simmons farm is part of our ranch now. It was located downriver from here, right along the banks. He thought that since the sounds had been heard under the ground, they may have been coming from the valley."

Skye broke in excitedly. "Down in the valley would have been under the ground in a roundabout way."

"Yes," Dad agreed. "And it would explain why the cry for help seemed to be muffled and far away. Poppy spent a good deal of time exploring the hills and caves in that area for some clue to Old Pete."

"Did he find anything?" Brooke quizzed.

"Not much. All he found was an old, torn shirt that might have belonged to Pete, but it was so weathered by that time there was no way to be sure."

Brooke stared into the silvery darkness of the night. Old Pete could be somewhere in those hills, maybe even hidden in a cave. Of course, she knew he'd be dead by now, but she could almost see him banging his axe on one of the walls of the limestone caves, calling out for help.

Dad put his hat back on. "Well, let's turn in for the night. Since we'll be checking the cows in a closer pasture tomorrow, we can sleep in a little. How does seven o'clock sound?"

"Um, good, Dad," Brooke yawned as she stood up. In the moonlight the trees cast dark shadows across her path as she walked with Skye to the cabin. She was tired, but she wasn't sure she'd be able to sleep. The story still clung in her mind like a fly trapped in a spider's web. What had happened to Old Pete?

In bed, Brooke listened for the usual night sounds, but it was quiet. Almost too quiet. It was as if the story of Old Pete had cast a spell over the whole valley. Eventually, she drifted off into an uneasy sleep.

Arooooo!

Brooke bolted up in bed at the eerie howl that disrupted her sleep. Only one kind of animal could make a sound like that.

Wolves.

Anxiously she looked at Dad. Why wasn't he waking up? Surely he must have heard them. Brooke listened, but Dad's snores were the only audible sound to be heard. Although they were noisy, they reminded her of a snorting pig more than a wolf. Brooke lay down. She must have imagined it. Her sleep had been restless, filled with chaotic dreams: Skye falling into a river of gold—Old Pete lost in a cave and unable to find his way out—and of she, herself, trying to rope a wolf. Brooke brushed the hair out of her eyes. Turning onto her side, a movement outside the window caught her eye. Fear gripped her heart in a stranglehold that held her breath captive. Part of the moonlight's silver glow was blotted out as a dark shadow paused in front of the window, peered inside and then vanished into the night.

Brooke screamed.

CHAPTER 15

"Huh? What? What's going on?" Dad croaked.

Brooke's hand quivered as she pointed to the window. Her teeth were rattling so hard she could barely talk. "I heard w-wolves howling and then s-s-something l-looked in the wi-window."

The cabin lit up in a soft white glow, as Dad climbed out of bed with the flashlight in hand. She waited with dread as he walked to the window. A chill surged through her body. What was out there? What had she seen?

Dad peered through the window. "Are you certain you saw something? Everything looks pretty quiet outside. Even Tuffy isn't too concerned." He pointed at Tuffy who was lying quietly by the door. "If there were wolves lurking around the cabin, he would be riled."

"I'm sure I did," she insisted. "It was black with pointy ears that stuck out the side of its head." She paused a moment trying to think of how to describe what she had seen. "It looked like your winter cap with the ear flaps that bounce up and down if you just let them hang loose." Brooke blinked rapidly as Dad shone the flashlight on her face.

"You think you saw a wolf out there with a winter cap on? In the middle of summer?" Dad chuckled. "Are you sure?"

Brooke heard a snicker from the bed above her. "Maybe it was Old Pete."

Brooke fumed silently. They didn't believe her. They thought it was just her imagination.

Dad shone the light on his watch. "Look, it's only three in the morning. If something was out there, it's probably gone by now. Let's try and get some sleep." Shutting the flashlight off, he climbed back into bed, and within a few minutes his snores rumbled through the cabin once more.

Frustrated, Brooke turned her back to the window and lay on her side. She was known for her sleepwalking and wild dreams, so she couldn't blame Dad for doubting her. Mom and Dad often locked the doors at night, but not to keep intruders out. They locked them to keep her in. Although she had no memory of it, they told her that once they had found the outside door standing wide open, two outside cats making a mess of Mom's kitchen, and Brooke sleeping outside curled up on a chair in her blanket. Brooke turned onto her back and looked out the moonlit window. Tonight had been different. She knew she had seen something out there, and she was going to prove it in the morning.

It seemed that she had barely closed her eyes when she opened them again and saw that sunlight had replaced the darkness of night. Brooke stretched her hands over her head and then sat up. Judging by the soft rumble above her and the low growl from behind her, Dad and Skye were still sleeping. Good. That would give her a chance to do some investigating. She slipped into her denim coat and pulled on her damp boots. As she tiptoed toward the door, a troublesome thought crept into her mind. What if the thing she saw last night was still out there? She nudged Tuffy awake. "Want to come along?"

Tuffy's stubbed tail wiggled back and forth as he stood up. Brooke opened the cabin door just wide enough to squeeze through, hoping to keep its piercing screech to a minimum. She crept through the small opening and whispered, "C'mon, Tuffy." He slipped through behind her and started to growl. In alarm, Brooke whirled around.

"Whoa! What are you guys doing here?" The words spilled from her mouth as she gawked at two black animals that peered at her from about twenty feet away. Looking past them, she spotted about ten more of various sized creatures scattered throughout camp. Tuffy continued to growl as Brooke reached down to pat his head.

"Easy, boy. They are only cows." Watching as their pointed ears moved slightly up and down while they lazily chewed their cud, the pieces began to fit together. "I bet I saw one of them last night." She went to the window and laughed out loud. Here was what she needed to prove she had not been seeing things. The proof was in the poop. Nothing else but a cow would leave behind such smelly evidence. Hearing the door screech open, Brooke rounded the corner, eager to tell someone what she had found.

"Well, isn't this just dandy?" Dad frowned as he put on his hat. "It looks like you were right, Brooke. You did see something last night, but to tell you the truth, I wish it hadn't been cows. I forgot about the cow that Skye saw on our first night here, and now we have a bigger problem."

The thrill of being proven right dampened when she saw Dad's disappointment. Cows in camp meant there was a break in the fence somewhere, and that meant more work. Also, with this many cows in one place, chances were there would be more of them wandering about.

"Brooke, wake up Skye and get the horses ready. I'll track these cows and see which direction they came from. I'll meet you back at the hitching rail." Dad started to walk away and then turned back. "And Brooke, hurry. I'd like to get these cows back into the fence and find that hole before the entire herd gets out."

"Sure, Dad." Turning to open the door, Brooke was startled when it screeched open on its own and met her outstretched hand.

Skye walked out of the cabin and pulled on her denim coat. "Did I hear Dad say something about cows being out?"

Brooke pointed at the small group of strays. "Yeah. There's a few of them."

"So you weren't just dreaming last night?"

"No, I wasn't," Brooke stated with a little bit of pleasure. At least finding the cows would keep Skye from teasing her about seeing ghosts. "Dad wants us to get the horses ready. Want a granola bar? We won't have time for breakfast." Brooke stepped

into the cabin and chose a box of raisin almond ones. She
stuffed two into her coat pocket and kept one out for eating.

"Sure. Toss me three."

Brooke sent three Skye's way and then pulled the wrapper
off the one in her hand. She took a big bite and said, "Wets go.
Ad wands uf oo urry."

Skye giggled. "In English, please."

Brooke swallowed. "Let's go. Dad wants us to hurry.
He would like to get these cows back in and the hole in the
fence repaired before the whole herd finds its way out." She
walked beside Skye to the tack room, careful to avoid the cow
droppings that dotted the ground. One misstep and her boots
would stink.

Brooke was bridling Jazz when she saw Dad come running
into camp. He startled the cows as he ran past, causing them to
scatter. Seeing his flushed face, Brooke knew something must
be wrong.

"I found another thirty head downriver. They are coming
this way." Dad huffed out a breath of air and then directed:
"Brooke, get the saddle bags that contain the fencing supplies
and put them on Jazz. Skye, get the medications. I'll get
Chocolate saddled."

Catching Dad's sense of urgency, Brooke darted to the tack
shed. She checked the plastic containers inside the saddle bags
to ensure they had staples and nails in them. They were full.
Slipping the hammer and fencing pliers into their pouches,
she picked up the bags and returned to Jazz. She eyed her rain
slicker tied to the back of her saddle. She would have to remove

it to get the saddle bags on, but she was unsure if she would have time to tie it back on. Dad was in a hurry. Looking up at the cloudless sky, she decided to take a chance that it wouldn't rain. She removed her rain slicker, tossed it inside the tack shed, and attached the fencing supplies to her saddle.

Dad mounted Chocolate. "Let's get these cows gathered up and headed down the river. Brooke, ride up to the corral and bring any cows that might be up there. Skye, you come with me."

Riding up to the corral, Brooke found two black cows with their calves. She rode Jazz around the far side of them and turned them toward the cabin. They bellowed loudly as they passed the tack room and joined the cows Dad and Skye were chasing out of the trees. Brooke had to laugh. Cows were very curious creatures. All it took was for one cow to moo loudly and the rest of the herd would rush in to see what was happening.

"Hey you, come back here." Brooke turned Jazz toward a calf that was trying to get away. Jazz matched his jump to the left and his cut to the right. A feeling of victory filled Brooke as the calf turned around and ran back to the herd of cows.

"Way to go, girl," she praised, reaching down to pat Jazz's neck. Very few things in life compared to being partnered with a good horse, and as each day passed, Brooke was increasingly convinced that Jazz was one of the best. Brooke followed the cows out of camp and down to the river. She was surprised to find the water was only a few inches above Jazz's knees. It was about six inches lower than it had been yesterday at this spot.

"Dad, what's happening to the water?" Brooke questioned as they splashed up onto the bank. The cows made their way along a narrow meadow that bordered the river and then they headed back down into the water.

Dad shook his head. "I don't understand it, Brooke. I wish I knew. It is dropping too quickly."

Rounding a bend in the river, the group that they were chasing began to bellow again, and Brooke saw another herd of cows coming toward them. She did a quick count and found that there were about sixty in this group. Either Dad had miscounted or a lot more cows had escaped.

"Watch that the cows don't scatter when they mix," Dad hollered over the noise. "Brooke, keep an eye on that left side."

Cuing Jazz into a trot to keep up to the cows, Brooke rode up along the left side of the herd. The cows were swirling in confusion, trying to decide which way to go. Brooke had Jazz pace back and forth along the edge of the herd to keep them grouped together. She could hear Tuffy barking somewhere in the chaos behind them, encouraging the cows to move back downriver. After a few minutes of disorder, the cows were headed back in the right direction.

A while later, Dad said, "We are close to the gate. You girls keep them going while I go ahead and get it open." He cued Chocolate into a trot, scattering a few of the cows along the edge as he went past.

Brooke sat confidently on Jazz, barely touching the reins as they worked together to turn a wandering calf back into the herd. A sense of accomplishment filled her. This cattle chase was so different from the one a couple of days ago. This time she and Jazz were working together as a team. The bond between them was growing because she could trust Jazz. This, in turn, enabled her to overcome her fears and ride with confidence. She cued Jazz into a lope as the cows broke into a run. They had spotted the open gate.

Brooke joined Skye in driving the last of the stragglers through the gate. "Funny how cows can be so glad to return to the fence they just broke out of."

"Yeah. It makes one wonder why they thought they had to get out in the first place."

Once the cows were in, Dad motioned for Brooke and Skye to come inside the fence. "It was not hard to find the hole," he said. "The cows knocked the gate down."

As she rode inside the fenced area, Brooke looked at the barbed-wire gate propped up against the fence. It appeared to be in good shape except for one broken post.

"Can you replace the post?" she asked. Posts kept the wires tight so they didn't sag to the ground. Without another good post in place, the cows might see the drooping wires as another chance to escape.

Dad pointed to a grove of small poplar trees next to the fence. "I can use one of those saplings. Here, Brooke. Take Chocolate while I get this gate fixed."

Brooke took hold of Chocolate's reins while Dad closed the gate and then removed the fencing tools from her saddle. He used the fencing pliers to remove the staples from the damaged post and tossed the broken pieces to the side. He walked into the group of young trees, and Brooke saw the top of one tree wave wildly back and forth before it snapped. A few minutes later Dad returned to the gate with a rugged tree post that was about five feet in height.

He retrieved some staples from the saddle bag and began to fasten the gate wires to the post. "I think I may know why the cows flattened the gate." He paused to pound in a staple. "I found some wolf tracks in the bush."

Brooke's heart skipped a beat. Wolves. Her dream. Was it possible she had heard them last night?

"There. Good as new." Dad returned the fencing supplies to Brooke's saddle and took back his reins. "While we're checking the cows today, keep an eye out for calves that look like they might be missing a mother, or any moms that appear to have lost a calf. I'm hoping we won't find anything and that the wolves were just passing through."

Brooke rode most of the day in peace. The sun's rays brought a glossy sheen to the grass, turning it emerald green. The purple aster flowers dipped their heads lightly in the wind as she rode through the hillside. The cows and calves seemed to be content. She hoped Dad was right and the wolves had just been passing through. Walking into the shade of a small collection of poplar trees, Brooke found a white-faced, black calf standing beside a rotten log. With his droopy ears and troubled breathing Brooke knew he would need treatment. The two black speckles under his right eye made it appear as if he was crying. She chased him out of the trees and into the grass so Dad would be able to rope him.

"Hey, Dad. Found one," Brooke yelled and waved across the meadow to where Dad was checking some other cows.

She followed the calf as he walked slowly toward a group of calves that were bunting heads. Compared to them this little calf looked like he was on the brink of death.

Dad made his way across the field to join her. He pointed to her rope. "Want to give it a try?"

Brooke looked at him in surprise.

"Well, you did rope your sister," Dad encouraged. "And this guy doesn't appear to be very energetic."

Brooke untied her rope from the saddle and readied her loop. Excitement surged through her veins. Her first calf, and what a perfect one to try on. He didn't have much energy. Even though he was nearing the rowdy group, he wasn't joining in their fun. He continued to trudge slowly through the grass. Her plan was to sneak up behind him and flip the loop over his head. Brooke smiled in anticipation. It couldn't get much easier than that, although she would have to be careful not to startle the boisterous band of calves. If she did, they would scatter and the sick one might follow. Brooke wasn't sure she could catch a calf in an all-out run. But a calf that was standing still or walking slow—that was manageable.

Gripping the coils of the rope in her left hand, Brooke hooked her reins on the smallest two fingers of the same hand. Taking the loop in her right hand, she turned Jazz toward the calf and kept her at a walk. At thirty feet away she spun the rope over her head to ensure it moved freely.

"Nooo!" Brooke muttered in frustration under her breath. So much for her plan. The movement of her rope had startled the group of calves, and now they were scampering in every direction. The sick calf seemed to have forgotten he was sick, for he was fleeing as quickly as the others.

Jazz moved into a lope and closed the distance. Brooke's heart galloped in time with Jazz's hooves as they pulled in behind the calf. Brooke leaned forward in the saddle, and as Jazz's nose came in line with the calf's hip, she twirled the rope over her head. One. Two. Three.

Brooke let the rope fly and watched it soar gracefully through the air. She waited in breathless expectation as it sailed straight for the calf.

She had him!

CHAPTER 16

She didn't have him.

Helpless to do anything but watch, Brooke saw the rope bounce off the back of the calf before plummeting to the ground. She slowed Jazz to a walk as the calf sped away. How could she have missed? Full of frustration she booted Jazz harshly in the sides. Jazz leaped forward, causing Brooke to yank back on the reins. Jazz's head flew up as she slid to a stop.

Brooke reached down to rub Jazz's neck, knowing she should not have taken out her frustration on her horse. She didn't stomach failure very well. "Sorry girl. It's not your fault, but I was so sure we had him."

Riding up beside her, Dad asked, "What happened?"

Brooke began to coil up the rope that lay empty on the ground. "I forgot to aim in front of the calf. I threw the rope for his head, but by the time it reached him, the loop bounced off his back and he got away."

"It is hard to remember everything at first, but with practice you'll get it." Dad pointed to the calf. "He didn't wander too far. Why don't you try again?"

Brooke eyed the calf that stood about fifty feet from her. That sprint must have drained his energy for he appeared to be more tired than before. His nose sagged to the ground while his sides heaved in and out. She knew she should try again. She would never be a cowgirl if she quit every time she ran into trouble.

She finished coiling her rope and trotted Jazz toward the calf. He took a few half-hearted steps as she spun the loop and let it go. It flew over his head and wrapped itself neatly around his neck. Jazz stopped as Brooke pulled the rope tight and dallied it around her saddle horn.

"I got him! I got him!" she exclaimed in victory. It had taken two attempts, but she had done it. She had roped her first calf.

Brooke held the rope tightly as Skye prepared to give the calf his medicine. He didn't flinch as the needle plunged into his neck and the amber liquid disappeared under his skin. When she was done, Skye pulled the rope off his neck and let it drop to the ground. The calf made no attempt to leave even though he was free.

Brooke watched him with concern as she coiled her rope and tied it to her saddle. "Do you think he'll be okay?"

"I think so," Dad said. "His mom will come for him once we're gone. Since we are done here, let's head back to the cabin."

Stopping at the river to let their horses drink, Brooke twisted around for one last glimpse of the little patient. A cow trotted up, sniffed him and then licked his neck. Walking a few steps away, she mooed gently to the calf and waited for him to catch up to her. Brooke watched as the pair slowly moved across the pasture. It seemed he would be all right.

"Does the river look lower than it was this morning?"

Brooke turned back at the troubled tone in Dad's voice. Glancing down at the water, she watched as it wound its way through Jazz's legs. It was two inches below her knees. This morning it had been above them.

"It is lower, but how can it be dropping so fast?" Brooke voiced the question, knowing there was no answer. What she did know was that without water, the ranch would be in serious trouble. She wished she could do something to help, but it wasn't as if she could make water magically appear.

That night as she sat by the fire with Dad and Skye, a band of eerie cries shattered the quiet stillness of the evening. Brooke knew that sound all too well. It was wolves. Far away at first, the howls came steadily closer. Tuffy growled, his fur standing up on end. Dad went to the cabin and returned with his rifle.

Even though the fire was warm, Brooke couldn't stop the quivers that swept through her body. Wolves terrified her. Across the river, she heard something large crash through the bush. The sinister snarls followed close behind, growing louder and then quieter as they headed past the camp and up the river. And then everything was quiet. Deathly quiet. Brooke almost bolted off her chair when Skye tapped her shoulder.

"Can I sit by you?" Skye asked timidly.

"Sure." Brooke scooted over on the log bench to make room, glad for the company. Skye squeezed in beside her and trembled slightly. Brooke understood why. In some ways, the silence was more unnerving than the noise of the chase. The lack of sound could mean the wolves had been successful in their hunt.

"What do you think they were chasing?" Skye whispered.

"I don't know. It could have been a deer or moose. Maybe even a cow. But whatever it was, I hope it got away." Brooke put her arm around Skye. In the flickering light she could see Skye's mouth droop downwards. She knew Skye had a soft spot in her heart for animals, and right now she was probably worried about the one the wolves had been chasing.

Dad's voice broke the heavy silence. "Why don't you girls get ready for bed? Sounds like things are quieting down, but I'm just going to stay out here for a while to make sure we don't get any unwanted visitors. I don't want those wolves to double back and get a horse."

Brooke gripped Skye's quivering hand as they walked to the outhouse before making their way to the cabin. She forced herself to take one step and then another into the dark trees. She tried to act brave for Skye, but it wasn't easy. Shuddering, Brooke waited outside the outhouse. What if the wolves had doubled back? She could almost feel their haunting yellow eyes watching her. She could almost see their snarling mouths opened wide, revealing their sharp, pointed teeth as they waited for her.

Brooke fought the urge to look over her shoulder. She kept telling herself there was nothing there, but finally she could fight it no longer. She peeked over her shoulder and then jumped back as a black shadow bounded toward her from the direction of the fire.

CHAPTER 17

"Oh, Tuffy. It's you!" Brooke felt her terror drain away as she knelt down and rubbed his head. Tuffy's stubbed tail began to wiggle and he licked her nose. Having him wait by her side gave her some confidence. He would alert her if the wolves were nearby. When Skye came out of the outhouse Brooke slipped inside. When she came out she was alone.

"Skye? Tuffy?" Brooke whispered anxiously. Where had they gone? She stared into the darkness to see if they were hiding in the shadows. It would be a mean trick to play on a night like tonight, but she wouldn't be surprised if Skye tried it.

Screeeech!

At the sound of a grinding squeak, she had her answer. They were already at the cabin. She walked back, thankful that she didn't have to worry about being ambushed along the way.

"Ewww!" Brooke cringed as she stepped into something soft and squishy. Hopefully that wasn't what she thought it was, but the foul stench that rose from her right foot told her otherwise. She tried to remove most of the mess from her boot before entering the cabin. Seeing that Skye and Tuffy were already inside, she didn't try to hide the sarcasm from her voice.

"Thanks for waiting!"

"I'm sorry, Brooke. I just got too scared." Skye wrinkled her nose. "What's that smell?"

"A pie freshly made, courtesy of the cows that were visiting this morning."

Skye snorted and then laughed. "Wasn't that kind of them to leave something behind for you to remember them by?"

Brooke snickered. "Yes it was. Are you sure you don't want some?" She slipped her boot off and held it out to Skye. "I'm sure it would be quite tasty!"

"No, I think I'll pass—yuck. That stuff really stinks. Maybe you should put your boot outside."

"My thoughts exactly." Brooke opened the door and set her boot beside the cabin. Pulling off her other boot, she slipped into tomorrow's clothes and climbed into bed. Listening to Skye get settled above her, she said, "Good night, Skye."

"G'night, Brooke."

The next morning, Brooke slowly climbed her way out of the land of dreams as someone nudged her shoulder back and forth.

"Wake up, sleepyhead. Breakfast is ready."

Brooke rubbed her eyes and sat up. Was it morning already? The smell of bacon in the air and the grinning face of Skye in front of her confirmed that it was.

"C'mon, get up. I have a surprise for you."

"Okay. Okay. Give me a minute." Brooke tightened up her ponytail, put her coat on, and began to pull on her boots.

"Yuck," she complained. Her right boot was soaking wet. What had happened? She looked at Skye's grinning face and knew she had something to do with it.

Brooke snarled in annoyance. "Is this your surprise? What did you do? You know I hate wet boots."

"What did I do?" Skye's face flushed red. "I thought I'd clean your boot for you—get rid of the stench. But right now something else stinks a lot worse." Skye slammed the door shut as she left the cabin.

Regret filled Brooke as she finished pulling on her wet boot. She had totally forgotten about her slip into the cow pie last night. Skye had done her a favor, and instead of being thankful, she had chewed her out. She was going to have to find Skye and apologize.

Walking to the food table, Brooke picked up a plate as Dad set the coffee pot on the fire. She was a little puzzled by the troubled frown on his face. Usually he had a smile first thing in the morning. Helping herself to two pancakes, she slathered them in syrup and then added three slices of bacon. She sat down beside Skye and felt a cold chill as Skye slid away from her. Brooke cleared her throat.

"Skye, I . . ."

"Does anyone want a drink?" Dad interrupted.

"Sure," Brooke answered. "Water please." Looking back at Skye, Brooke began her apology again. "Skye, I'm sorry. I totally forgot that my boot was dirty. Thanks for cleaning it." When Skye didn't say anything, Brooke lifted a piece of bacon out of her plate and took a bite. Without anyone talking, the silence was almost deafening. Even Boots was silent.

Brooke looked up into the trees. "Where's Boots?" she wondered out loud. Perhaps with the commotion of yesterday morning he had left to find a new home. She glanced at Skye to see if she had any ideas, but Skye continued to give her a cold shoulder.

Dad joined them and handed Brooke a cup. "Here's your water," he said.

Brooke took the cup from his outstretched hand. "Ouch! That's hot!" She jumped up and dropped the mug. Hot liquid splashed onto her pants and boots. She picked up the mug, sniffed inside and looked at Dad in confusion. "Dad, you brought me coffee."

"What?" Dad took the cup back and chuckled. "Sorry honey. My mind was on other things. I'll get some water."

"Looks like this is your morning for wet boots," Skye commented.

"Yeah, and the day is just beginning," Brooke answered dryly. At least one good thing had resulted from her wet boots. Skye was speaking to her again. Brooke turned her focus back to Dad and watched as he filled the mug with water. What was on his mind? It must be serious if he never even noticed that he had brought her coffee instead of water. Maybe there was trouble with the cows again. She took the cup of water Dad offered her, and asked, "Which fence are we checking today?"

Dad was quiet for a moment before he answered. "I think we will go check the cows up river. I had planned to finish the last pasture down river, but the level of water has dropped by another six inches since last night. Something has to be blocking the water flow. I want to see if we can find it."

Brooke kept her eyes on Dad as she finished eating. She had never seen him like this before, and it worried her. She could feel his fear. After cleaning up breakfast, Brooke filled the saddle bags with lunch and walked with Skye to the tack room. Dad had the horses saddled and tied to the hitching rail, ready to go. Brooke attached the bags with the lunch onto her saddle, and Skye took the medication bag with her on Indee.

At the first river crossing, Brooke was surprised to see rocks peeking out of the surface of the water. She would be able to jump from rock to rock and make it across without getting wet. All her comments about the river disappearing came back to her. At the beginning of the week it seemed impossible. Now it was like someone had shut off the tap to the Silverton River, and it was drying up before her eyes. No wonder Dad was worried.

The day sped by, and Brooke was glad when Dad said they should stop and let their horses have a bite to eat. Most of the day had been spent looking for what might be blocking the river, but all they found was two beaver dams which were not big enough to stop the flow of water. There had to be another reason why the river was drying up, but she didn't have any clue as to what that might be. What made a river disappear?

Brooke slid to the ground and stretched her legs. After so many hours in the saddle, it felt good to walk around.

"We're going to water our horses," Dad said. "Want to come?"

"No, go ahead. I watered Jazz a little bit ago." As Dad and Skye left with their horses, Brooke found her attention snagged by a bright orange butterfly that fluttered past her head. She followed it with her eyes as it flew toward a lone spruce tree that stood in the middle of the pasture. Shielding her eyes from the sun, Brooke took a few steps forward to the tree. Standing there in the shade of the prickly branches was a lone calf. His head hung low and she could see that his breathing was labored. Another patient to treat. As she returned to Jazz and climbed into the saddle, a wild idea made its way into her mind.

What if she had the calf roped when Dad and Skye returned? Wouldn't they be surprised?

She pulled her rope free, made her loop, and took a couple of swings over her head. She was ready. Turning toward the calf, she said, "All right, Jazz. Let's get him."

The calf caught sight of them and began to flee. Brooke leaned forward in the saddle, her gaze focused on the calf. The meadow surrounding them passed in a blur as she and Jazz moved as one across the field. The wind rushed past her face as the gap narrowed. Forty feet. Thirty feet. Twenty feet. She began to twirl the rope and as soon Jazz's head was even with the hip of the calf, she aimed for the empty space in front of him and released the rope. The calf tried to run through the loop, but it tightened around his neck.

"Dally! Dally! Dally!" Dad yelled above the bawling of the calf.

Jazz slid to a stop as Brooke wrapped the rope twice around the saddle horn and held on tight. The calf spun around, fighting hard. He twisted his head back and forth struggling to get free. When that didn't work, he charged circles around Jazz. Jazz spun with him, keeping her head pointed at him the whole time.

"Wow, Brooke!" Dad exclaimed as he rode up. "You caught a feisty one." He pulled out his rope and threw the loop onto the ground under the calf's stomach. As soon as his back feet were in the loop, Dad pulled the rope tight, binding the back legs of the calf. Chocolate backed up until the calf tipped over on his side. That seemed to knock the fight out of him. After Skye had treated him, Brooke loosened the rope from her saddle horn so that Skye could slip it off the calf's head. Once Skye was on Indee, Chocolate walked forward and scared the calf so he jumped up. Dad's rope slid off his legs as he ran away to find his mother.

"Well done, Brooke," Dad praised. "It looks like I have a new roping partner."

Brooke's hands shook as she coiled up her rope. Dad's roping partner. That had been her wish for so long. Now that she was acting with courage instead of letting fear hold her back, her dream of being a cowgirl was coming true.

"That's another day," Dad said. "Let's get back. I'm getting hungry."

Brooke tied her rope to the saddle and followed the others down the trail that led to camp. She could almost see the old cabin when Tuffy began to bark excitedly. He sniffed the rocks around the horses' feet, seeming to catch the scent of something, then darted across the river. He continued to bark on the other side.

"Tuffy! Come back here," Dad yelled. "That crazy dog. He's always chasing something." He waited for a minute and then said, "It doesn't look like he's coming back, so we had better go see what he's found. Hopefully it's not more cows."

When they had crossed the river and walked into a canopy of trees, Brooke saw Tuffy running in circles and sniffing the ground. He ran further into the bush and barked again. Dad jumped off Chocolate, handed his reins to Brooke, and followed Tuffy. A few minutes later, Dad reappeared.

"Tie your horses up and follow me," he said. Brooke saw him pick up some leaves, smell them, and then throw them back to the ground. She tied Jazz and Chocolate to separate trees and followed Dad deeper into the forest.

"Remember all that noise we heard last night?" Dad asked.

Brooke glanced at Skye and nodded. How could she forget? Scanning the area before her, she noticed that the covering of dead leaves on the ground had been disturbed. As well, a few of the poplar saplings were laying twisted and broken.

"I think there was a fight here last night. There's blood here and here." Dad pointed to the ground in two places. Bending down, he said, "I'm quite certain those wolves must have been chasing a moose."

Brooke knelt beside Dad. On the ground she saw what looked like a large upside down heart, split down the middle. It was a moose track. Close beside it was the large paw print of a wolf. She brushed a few of the leaves out of the way, and cringed at what she found: a smaller reflection of the large moose track. It had to belong to a moose calf.

"Oh, no," Skye cried out, kneeling down beside Brooke. "Not a baby."

Crawling on her hands and knees, Brooke continued to brush more leaves out of the way. She found one track and then another. Each one led further away from the place of the battle.

Tuffy barked behind them and ran deeper into the forest.

"You girls wait here," Dad ordered. "I'll go see what Tuffy found."

Brooke nodded and turned her attention back to the calf tracks. They pointed toward a low hedge of bushy green-leafed trees. Brooke stared at the shrubs, trying to spot anything that might be hidden within, but the intertwined branches blocked her sight.

"Brooke, do you think the calf might be in there?" Skye whispered.

Brooke shrugged her shoulders. She knew wild animals would often hide their young in one place and then run in an opposite direction in an effort to draw predators away from their young. She peered at the bushes. The fight had been last night. Surely a calf wouldn't still be hiding in there.

Skye started to crawl forward, but Brooke put her hand on her shoulder. "Skye, let's wait . . ." Brooke's voice faltered. Did that bush just move?

"Did you see that?" Skye hissed in Brooke's ear.

Brooke nodded, her gaze fixed on the trembling leaves as the branches once again shivered with movement.

"Something's in there," Skye whispered anxiously.

"Skye, let's . . . get out . . ." Brooke broke off her sentence, panic choking off her words. She watched in terror as twigs snapped and the bushes seemed to come to life.

"Skye, look out!"

CHAPTER 18

BROOKE GRABBED SKYE'S SHOULDER AND YANKED her out of the path of the stampeding creature. Out of the corner of her eye, Brooke saw a brown blur rush past them as they tumbled into the leaves.

Brooke pulled herself up onto her knees and spun around. If that creature was coming back for a second attack she wanted to be ready.

"It's the calf moose," Skye said in a hushed, but excited tone. "He's alive." She started to slowly crawl toward it.

"What are you doing?" Brooke whispered harshly.

"I'm going to see if I can catch it."

Brooke's voice went up a notch. "Catch it? Are you crazy?"

"Not so loud! You will scare the poor thing. Look at him. Do you really think he's going to hurt me?"

Brooke turned her focus on the calf moose and had to admit he did not look very dangerous. It stood on four pencil-thin legs. His hips jutted out under his chocolate-brown hair. He had a jumbo-sized nose and sorrowful, black eyes. If any animal could look heartbroken, this one did. But that didn't change the fact that he was a young wild animal whose mother might be nearby.

"What about his mom? If she finds us with her baby, she'll turn nasty," Brooke warned. Dad had advised them many times to be careful around wild animals and their babies. It was especially important not to get between a mother and her offspring. Most mothers would do anything to protect their young.

"If the wolves were chasing her, she might be dead," Skye replied fervently. "Look at him, Brooke. He's starving."

Brooke looked at the scrawny, quivering calf. He did look hungry, but that didn't change the fact that his mother might be around. "At least wait until Dad gets back," Brooke cautioned. Sometimes Skye acted with her heart instead of her head.

"All right. I'll wait," Skye muttered.

Brooke glanced into the woods, hoping Dad would soon return. Getting Skye to be patient and wait was like trying to keep an excited dog on a leash. It would only work for so long. She was relieved when Dad emerged from the trees.

"What do we have here?" He walked forward a few steps and stopped. "The moose calf. It's a good thing you found him. His mother won't be coming back."

"She's dead?" Skye whimpered.

Dad nodded. "I'm surprised he survived. His mother must have hid him well and then ran into the bush to try and draw the wolves away. She probably planned to return for him, but the wolves got to her before she could make it back."

"What are we going to do? We can't leave him here," Skye said forcefully. "What if the wolves come back? Who will protect him?"

"We'll have to take him with us. He won't stand a chance out here on his own. Let's form a triangle around him." Dad motioned with his arms for Brooke to stand to his right and Skye to his left. "Crouch low and slowly move toward him. He might try to make a run for it, so make sure you're ready if he comes your way. We might only have one chance at this," Dad advised. "If he runs into the bushes, we may not find him again."

Moving to Dad's right, Brooke bent down and held out her hands in front of her. She walked in time with Dad and Skye, matching them step for step as they moved toward the calf. As the distance grew smaller, the moose began to tremble violently. He looked wildly around the triangle, and Brooke cringed as his eyes locked on hers. In that second she knew he had decided she was the weak link.

He bolted straight toward her. Brooke leaped forward, trying to catch him around his neck. She missed. Her fingers vibrated as they slipped over his ribs. Grasping at his back legs she managed to take hold of one of his ankles. Brooke locked her fingers together and hung on tightly. She couldn't lose him.

"Help!" Brooke cried out. Tuffy came to her side and barked frantically. "Tuffy, go away," she yelled, gritting her teeth.

That wasn't the kind of assistance she needed. The moose was jerking his foot so violently that each jolt felt like it could yank her arms out of their sockets. How could such a small creature have such a powerful kick?

"I'm here." Skye wrapped her arms around the moose's chest and rump.

Brooke held on as the kicks became weaker. "Can you hold him?"

"I think so. He is not fighting anymore. He's tired out."

Brooke let go of the ankle so the moose could put his foot back on the ground. "It's no wonder he's weak. I doubt he's eaten since we heard the wolves last night. That is a long time for him to go without food." She began to scratch his back by his hips. His hair was so soft and thick it felt like velvet. The calf turned his head toward her. His ears slumped downwards as he let out a soft squeak. He looked so sad Brooke thought he might cry.

"I think he misses his mom," Skye said.

"He's quite small to be on his own." Brooke peered around the small opening where they were standing. "Do you know where Dad went? I thought he would be here helping us."

"When he saw we had the moose, he said he was going to get Chocolate."

"I must have missed that in all the commotion. Is he going to try to carry the moose on his saddle?"

"I think that is the plan. It should work. He does it all the time with regular calves if they can't travel far on their own."

Brooke jumped when she saw something large and brown emerge from the bushes to her right.

Skye giggled. "It's just Chocolate."

Brooke felt her face turn red. "I know. It just startled me. For a split second I thought it could be the mother moose coming back."

Dad brought Chocolate to a stop and called out, "Bring that little fellow over here. He's going to get his first pony ride."

"Brooke, you take that side of him," Skye directed. "If we keep him in between us he shouldn't be able to get away."

Brooke stood opposite Skye and helped her shuffle the moose in Dad's direction. She was about to offer to lift the orphan up to Dad when Chocolate suddenly reared. Brooke tightened her grip on the moose as Chocolate's hooves pawed the air.

"Quick, Skye. Back up." Brooke pulled the calf out of the range of Chocolate's hooves.

"Whoa, boy. Easy. Easy," Dad urged.

From a safe distance Brooke watched as Dad pulled on the reins, fighting for control. As Chocolate's front feet touched the ground, he tried to bolt. But Dad spun him in circles, causing his hooves to churn up the dead leaves on the ground. Finally, Chocolate came to a standstill. His eyes were large as he watched the moose. Dad backed him up a few paces and then tied him to a tree. "So much for that idea," he commented dryly. "Looks like we'll have to go to plan B."

Brooke laughed. "I didn't know a baby moose could be so scary."

"I didn't either." Dad strode over and picked the moose up in his arms. The calf kicked his spaghetti-like legs back and forth, making it look like he was swimming in midair. He struggled for a few seconds and then sat limply in Dad's arms.

"All right, let's get to camp before he decides to try something else. Make sure you—oh yuck!" Dad jumped backwards as a stream of liquid shot out from under the moose.

Brooke snorted as she covered her mouth with her hand in an effort to hold her laugh in. Dad's jeans were soaked.

"Hey, it's not funny," Dad scowled. "Getting a bath from the moose was not what I signed up for. He's proving to be quite a handful. Maybe I should just leave him here."

"Dad," Skye protested.

"Just kidding, honey. I won't leave him. But you'd think he could have shown a little gratitude." Dad grinned. "C'mon, let's get to camp before something else happens."

As they made their way to camp, Brooke led Chocolate while she rode Jazz. Dusk was creeping up on the horizon, painting the sky burnt orange with streaks of purple and red slashed through it. She was glad the day was winding down. It had been a long one.

"You girls put the horses away, and bring some hay for the moose to lie down on," Dad instructed. "I'll rig up some kind of fence to keep him in."

After taking care of the horses, Brooke joined Skye in grabbing a couple of armfuls of hay. She was pleased to see the cheery fire when they reached the cabin.

Brooke dropped her armload of hay into the log stump fence Dad was just completing. "What do you think we should call him?"

Skye added her hay to the pile. "What do you think of Morris?"

"Morris the moose." Brooke thought about his big nose and skinny legs. She didn't know why, but the name Morris seemed to suit him. "I like it," she agreed as she fluffed the dried grass stalks into a bed for Morris. "His bed is ready. Now we just have to add the moose."

"Morris," Skye corrected. "Dad, where is he?"

Dad put the last stump in place. "I tied him by the cabin. I'll go get him."

"I hope he likes his new home," Brooke said as Dad returned from the cabin. Morris hung like a limp towel in his arms. "Is he alive?"

Dad laid Morris on the hay bed. "He's is, but he's very weak. I called Mom on the mobile and asked her to get in touch with the vet to see if we can feed him the same powered milk replacer we give to the orphan calves." He stood up. "Now if you will keep an eye on him, I will go change and then get supper ready while we wait for Mom to arrive."

Brooke stooped down beside the fence and stroked Morris's head. She could see the outline of every bone under his skin. Right now the fattest part of him appeared to be his nose.

Skye knelt down. "He looks so lifeless. I hope he'll be okay. Life hasn't been easy for him so far."

A short time later, Brooke saw a white flash of light splash along the bottom of the trees as Mom rumbled into camp with the diesel truck. After the engine was shut off, Mom's silhouette was visible as she passed in front of the lights before they flashed off. She had a milk bottle in her right hand.

She gave the bottle to Brooke. "Careful. The bottle is full. The vet said the milk replacer should be just fine for our little orphan. We need to feed him about two pints every three to four hours."

Brooke climbed into the fence and attempted to get Morris to drink. When she tried to put the bottle into his mouth, he began to thrash his head from side to side. "Skye, could you help me?" she asked. Once Skye had a firm grasp of his head, Brooke made another attempt to feed him, but this time Morris clamped his mouth shut.

"Maybe you should squirt some milk on your fingers and put them in his mouth," Skye suggested. "It might help him to think about eating instead of fighting."

Brooke did as Skye recommended. She giggled at the feel of his slobbery tongue wrapping itself around her fingers. "It tickles, but it seems to be working. He is sucking my finger." She placed another few drops of milk on her fingers and placed them into his mouth. Eventually she slipped the nipple into his mouth and removed her fingers. Morris began to drink. He started off slowly, but gained speed, emptying the bottle in a short time.

Brooke pulled the nipple out of his mouth and watched as his muscles began to quiver. "Looks like the milk is warming him up. He's shaking just like a calf."

Skye released his head. "Well, he is a calf. He's just different looking."

Brooke looked at Skye. "Thanks for your help. I'm surprised he found the energy to fight."

Skye nodded. "Hopefully it will be easier next time."

"You girls want to come and have some food?" Dad called out.

Skye's stomach growled loudly, and Brooke laughed as they went to eat. "Sounds like Morris isn't the only one who is hungry!"

Before bed, Brooke helped Skye feed Morris once more, and Mom helped Dad move his fence to the front of the cabin. She was going to spend the night with them. Tuffy lay down beside Morris. Brooke knelt down and rubbed his head. Tuffy was a good dog. He seemed to understand when people or animals needed help.

The next morning, Brooke awoke before anyone else was up, so she slipped outside. A quick check revealed that Morris had made it through the night and was resting peacefully. She shivered as a light, cool wind brushed against her face. Even the rays of the sun breaking over the top of the valley did little to take the chill away. In the distance, she heard the crash of thunder. Would today bring rain? Since the view of the sky was limited at the cabin, she walked to the river to get a better look at the horizon.

Upon reaching the river, Brooke scanned the skyline. With the exception of a few puffy clouds, it was clear, but that didn't mean a storm wasn't lurking somewhere behind the hillside. Lowering her gaze, she cast an eye up and down the river banks and stumbled backwards in shock at the sight before her.

She couldn't believe it.

The river had disappeared.

CHAPTER 19

IN SHOCK, BROOKE SQUEEZED HER EYES shut, unable to believe what she had just seen. It must be an illusion. Or maybe she was sleepwalking through a baffling, terrifying dream. Rivers couldn't disappear overnight. It was impossible.

Wasn't it?

Peeking out from behind her eyelids, Brooke peered at the scenery before her. To her disappointment, it had not changed. Kneeling down, her fingers brushed the damp sand no longer hidden by the sparkling stream.

This wasn't her imagination or a dreadful dream.

This was reality.

It was as if the earth had opened wide its mouth and sucked the river dry. Stripped of its shimmering beauty, the river bed lay unprotected and bare. Small puddles were the only remnants of the rippling waters. The river's heart—that which brought joy, music and life—had silently disappeared in the night. Brooke felt her heart tighten within her. She understood what that was like. When Buckshot had died, a part of her life had slipped away. She had once felt like the river now looked. Empty and dry.

Thunder rumbled once again. Brooke wrapped her arms around herself as a gust of wind swept past. She glanced into the sky. The white, cottony clouds raced cheerfully on the wings of the wind, seemingly unaware of the threatening storm that was gathering behind the hills, hidden from sight. Standing up, Brooke trembled inwardly. What would happen to the ranch? To the cows? Neither would be able to survive without water.

Turning her back on the desolate scene, she hurried up the gentle slope toward the cabin. She had to get Dad. He would know what to do. Glimpsing a flash of movement by the cabin door, she hollered, "Dad! Come quick!" Drawing closer, she realized it was not Dad who was outside. It was Morris. Their spindly-legged guest was attempting to flee. He rammed the far side of the fence. Two stumps wobbled.

In alarm she exclaimed "Morris, no!" as he butted the fence once again. The two stumps rocked back and forth before toppling onto their sides. He scrambled over them and darted toward the trees.

Brooke shifted into high gear and raced past the cabin, leaping over an overturned log that had rolled into her path. That crazy creature was quick! If she didn't catch him before he gained more momentum, it would be too late. Thrusting out her arms, she clutched at one of his back legs. Feeling the velvet fur, she locked her fingers and struggled to keep her grip as he strained forward, fighting to get away.

In desperation she cried out, "Help! Someone, help me!"

Morris began to kick furiously, jerking her arms in chaotic circles. She heard the cabin door screech. Whoever was coming better get here soon! She could feel her fingers slipping. This pint-sized moose had gained a lot of strength since yesterday. She snuck a quick peek over her shoulder, relieved to see Dad was on his way.

"Hang on, Brooke. I'm almost there."

Brooke bit her bottom lip as her hands slipped a little further. She was losing him. Her fingertips grasped the top of his slippery hoof and then slid off. She lost her balance and stumbled to the ground, landing on her hands and knees. Raising her head, she saw Morris continue his mad dash for the trees.

Dad rushed past. "Not so fast, little fellow!" He got hold of the runaway and picked him up in his arms.

Brooke stood up, brushing the dirt and pine needles from her pants. That had been close. Thankfully Morris was still safe, although he didn't look too pleased about it. He continued to struggle in Dad's arms as they returned to the cabin. "It's a good thing you got here when you did, Dad. I couldn't hold onto him any longer."

"Was he loose when you got up?"

"No. I think I spooked him when I ran back from the river, but I . . ."

"What were you doing running back from the river, Brooke?"

"I . . ."

"Morris is a wild animal and any sudden movements will startle him," Dad lectured.

"But, I . . ."

"If he would have made it to the trees, we may have never found him. What would have happened to him then?"

"But, Dad . . ."

"I don't want to hear any excuses, young lady. You need to think before you act. Look at the trouble your actions caused."

Brooke scowled in frustration. She had been thinking— about the river. That's why she had been running in the first place. If Dad would just let her speak, he'd understand. She tried again.

"Dad, the . . ."

Screech.

The cabin door crashed open and Skye bolted outside, causing Morris to jump in Dad's arms.

Dad cautioned. "Slow down, Skye. He escaped once today already."

Skye patted her hands over Morris' body. "What happened? Is he hurt?"

"No, he's fine. Why don't you climb into the fence? You can hold him while I get his bottle ready." Dad placed Morris into her arms, set up the two overturned stumps, and stepped inside the cabin.

"Dad, wait," Brooke pleaded. Dad turned around. Both eyebrows were ready to slide down his nose. He was not happy, but she pushed ahead.

"The river's gone."

He took a step forward. "What did you say?"

Now that she had his attention, she had to help him understand. Maybe if she spoke slowly. "The. River. Is. Gone."

Dad's eyebrows went from a nosedive to a high jump in one movement, disappearing under his hat. "Gone?"

"Yes. That is what I have been trying to tell you. When I went down to the river this morning, the water was gone. There are only a few puddles left."

Brooke was only a few steps behind Dad as he ran to the river. He looked up and down the banks just as she had. He threw his hat to the ground and began to pace back and forth.

"What are you going to do?"

"I don't know. I really don't know. Although the water was low, I didn't think that it would stop flowing. Not once have I witnessed anything like this."

Brooke kicked at the ground, scattering the rocks. She had never seen Dad act this way before. He was the one that always had answers and knew what to do. He was a rock, undisturbed by troubles.

Until today.

Now he was worried. Uncertain. Without answers. Although she was unsure if she should, Brooke posed one more question that was burning in her mind.

"Will the cows be okay?"

Dad picked up his hat and shoved it back on his head. "They will be for the short term. There should be enough water in the low areas and the beaver dams to last for a while. And it would help if we got some rain."

Brooke remembered the thunder she had heard earlier in the morning. Maybe it would come in this direction. "What will happen once the pools dry up?"

Dad put his arm around her shoulder. "If that happens, we will be in big trouble. Our summer pasture is in these hills. We need all the crops and grass that are in the fields for winter feed. If we move the cows out of the river valley so they can drink at the watering holes that are in the fields, they'll eat the winter feed in the summer and we won't have anything to give them when winter comes."

"Couldn't we just buy more food for them?"

Dad shook his head. "Feed for that many cows would be too expensive. We could always sell some cows if we needed to, but if the river is actually gone for good . . ." Dad's voice trailed off.

Despair settled in, filling Brooke with a sense of hopelessness. She understood what Dad wasn't saying.

If the river was gone for good she could say good-bye to the Silver Valley Ranch as she knew it.

CHAPTER
20

BROOKE SNUCK SILENTLY AROUND THE SIDE of the cabin and ducked under the window. Dad was inside talking to Mom. She wanted to hear what they were saying. Eavesdropping wasn't a habit, but the future of the ranch was on the line.

"Ahhhh!"

Covering one ear and pressing the other against the weather-worn log, Brooke tried to block out all other sounds so she could concentrate on the muffled voices coming through the cabin wall. It sounded like someone was crying.

"Uh! Ouch!"

Brooke frowned. That was too loud to be coming from inside the cabin.

"Maaa!"

Something wasn't right. Crouching low until she was past the window, Brooke hastened to the front of the cabin.

"Morris, stop," Skye pleaded.

"Maaa!" Morris bawled as he struggled within her arms.

"Oh, Brooke. Can you help me?" Skye begged. "I'm scared if I let go he's going to run off again."

"Sure, what do you need?"

"Can you get his milk? The bottle is inside the cabin."

Brooke grasped the door handle. This was perfect. Now that she had a reason to go inside, she would hear what Dad and Mom were saying.

"Brooke, hurry, please!"

The usual screech filled the air as Brooke swung the door open, but then silence met her ears as she entered the cabin. She paused, feeling uncomfortable as Mom and Dad stared at her. Did they know she had been trying to listen in on their conversation?

"Um, hi!" Brooke stammered. "I'm just getting the bottle." She scanned the interior and spotted it sitting by the right side of the door. She picked it up and slipped outside.

"Brooke."

She halted at the ominous tone of Dad's voice. Returning inside, shame threaded its way around her chest, tightening like a saddle cinch around a horse. Now she was in trouble. She should never have tried to listen in on their talk.

Dad watched her with one eyebrow raised. "Don't you need the milk powder?"

"Oh, right. W-w-where is it?" Brooke stuttered. They had not figured out her secret . . . yet.

"It's on the floor by your feet," Dad answered, suspicion filling his voice. "Brooke, are you okay? Is there something else you want to tell us?"

"No! I'm fine! Everything's good." Brooke sputtered the words and snatched up the ice cream pail that contained the milk powder. She retreated from the cabin before they could ask any more questions. Whew! That had been close.

Reaching the cooker, she lifted the lid. Tiny waves of steam twirled upwards as the warm water glugged into the bottle. Once it was filled to the halfway point, she placed one scoop of milk powder in it and attached the nipple. The white powder dissolved as she sloshed the water back and forth.

Retracing her steps, she held out the bottle. "Here's your breakfast, Morris." He leaped forward, nearly bumping the bottle from her hands. She struggled to hang on as he ran his nose and tongue over it until he found the nipple. Wrapping his tongue around it, he began to drain its contents with a frenzy. As he drank, white foam bubbles formed around his mouth and dropped to the ground. Brooke observed, "It sure didn't take him long to figure out where his food comes from."

"He caught on really fast. Thanks for bringing the bottle, Brooke," Skye said in appreciation. "He was getting so wild, I was worried I might lose him."

Brooke held the bottle firmly as Morris drained the last drops of milk. At the sound of air whistling through the nipple, she pulled it from his mouth. "You know, he likes his bottle so much, if he did get away you might be able to use it as bait to catch him."

Skye's eyes widened in excitement. "And if that worked, I could teach him to lead by just having him follow the bottle."

"You want to halter break him?" Brooke rubbed Morris' head. His long tongue reached up, searching her hand for more milk.

"I'd like to, if I can convince Dad to keep him."

Brooke lifted her hand and wiped the slobber on her pants. "It would be pretty neat to have a pet moose," she agreed as the cabin door screeched open once again, this time announcing Mom and Dad's presence.

"Alright, here's the plan," Dad stated. "Although we are not done checking the cows, we need to leave camp today. The water in the river will only last for a short period of time. I have to find out what happened to it and hopefully find a way to get the water back. If that doesn't work I will need to decide what we are going to do with the cows."

Perplexed, Brooke turned her gaze to the barren riverbed. Did he think the river was playing a game of hide and seek? Where would a river go to hide? Searching for it would be like hunting for a butterfly in winter. It would be nearly impossible. The Silverton River wound its way through many miles of valleys and forests before it reached the Silver Valley Ranch.

Skye hugged Morris around the neck. "Can we take this little guy home?"

"You bet. Mom and I will take him with us when we go up to the house. The vet and the game warden should be dropping by later on today."

"The game warden?" Skye questioned. "Why is he coming?"

Dad explained. "There are times when an animal is orphaned, the game warden will grant special permission for someone to look after it."

Skye's voice squeaked. "You mean we might be able to keep Morris?"

Brooke almost laughed out loud. Skye sounded like a mouse who had just found a platter of cheese. And in a way maybe she had. This was what she was hoping for.

"It is possible, but it will be up to the warden," Dad repeated.

"Do you think they might say no?"

"They could."

"But I'd take good care of him," Skye pleaded.

"I know you would, honey. I wish the decision were up to me, but it isn't. We'll just have to wait and see."

Brooke watched as Skye's face saddened. She had a special love for animals, especially those in need. If a calf lost its mother, she was the one who volunteered to look after it. She poured so much love into them that they remembered her for years afterwards. She could walk up to them in an open field and pet them even after they had calves of their own.

Dad continued with his instructions. "Brooke and Skye, I need you to bring the horses. Take the road. It will mean extra miles, but it will be easier to lead Chocolate out that way instead of following the narrow trail that we took to get here. Since I'm uncertain of when we'll be coming back, I don't want to leave the horses in the corral, especially with wolves around."

"Okay," Brooke agreed. Horses locked in a fence would make an easy target for hungry wolves.

"Dad, couldn't I go up with Morris?" Skye requested hopefully. "I could look after him until the warden comes. Maybe if he saw how much Morris likes me, he'd let him stay."

Dad shook his head. "Brooke can't lead Indee and Chocolate out on her own. It's over a four hour ride, and since I can't go with her, you'll have to."

Brooke saw the tip of Skye's nose turn red. Uh, oh! That was a sure sign that she was unhappy. Skye looked at her and motioned with her head toward Dad. Confused, Brooke shrugged her shoulders. Skye frowned and jerked her head more insistently in Dad's direction. Brooke didn't know what to do. It was obvious Skye wanted her to say or do something, but she couldn't understand what it was.

"If you girls get your horses saddled, Mom and I will get your gear out of the cabin, and I'll throw some jerky and apples into the saddle bags for you."

After he disappeared into the cabin, Brooke stepped quickly to catch up to Skye. "Hey, wait up! What were you trying to tell me?" She watched as Skye wordlessly snatched Indee's lead rope and halter from the tack room, shot her a glare that could freeze water, and silently stomped off to the corral. Unsure of what she had done to tick Skye off, Brooke took ropes and halters for Jazz and Chocolate, and followed.

When she reached the wooden gate of the corral, Brooke saw that Skye already had Indee haltered. Opening the gate for her, Skye brushed past. Brooke jumped out of the way to avoid being run over by Indee.

Brooke caught hold of Jazz and Chocolate and buckled their halters on. "This should be a fun trip," she murmured as she led the two horses down to the hitching rail. It looked like Indee was on the receiving end of Skye's frustration as well, and he did not appear to be enjoying it. His ears were pinned back as Skye brushed him with quick, hard strokes.

"Hey . . ." Brooke started, and then interrupted herself. She was going to ask Skye to toss the brush over when she was done with it, but decided against it. With the mood Skye was in, she might end up with the brush right between the eyes. Instead, she went to the tack room and got her own brush. As she walked out, Skye swept in, pushing Brooke sideways so that she almost fell to the ground.

"Hey, watch it. You did that on purpose," Brooke fumed as she regained her balance.

"So? That's nothing compared to what you just did," Skye retorted. She yanked her saddle off its rack, and stomped out the door.

As Brooke brushed the dirt from Jazz's back, she deliberated on what to do. She knew it was in her best interests to let Skye cool off before asking her what was wrong. On the other hand, if they had to ride home together it might be better to get it out now. Deciding on the second option, she asked, "Skye, what did I do?"

"What did you do?" Skye snapped. "You could have told Dad that you would lead the horses up on your own. Now, because I have to go with you, I won't be there when the game warden comes, and Morris might be gone before we get back."

Brooke finished brushing Jazz and started on Chocolate. She should have known the trouble would have to do with Morris.

"It's a long trip, Skye. It would be safer for Indee if you rode him."

"You would be on the road," Skye opposed. "You could do it."

Brooke marched up to Skye and stared into her eyes. "And what if I had trouble and one of the horses got away?" She paused, and then added, "What if Indee got away?" Hopefully that would make Skye stop and think.

"He would just run home."

"And what if his lead rope got tangled. What would happen then?" She let her words sink in for a moment and then turned around. It was quiet as she saddled Jazz. She hoped that meant Skye was thinking about the dangers of a horse running loose in the hills, dragging a lead rope behind him. A trailing lead rope could become entangled around a branch, tree, rock, or even the horse's own leg. If the horse became ensnared and was unable to get free, he would be an easy target for wild animals—especially wolves. That was a risk Brooke wasn't willing to take.

She had already lost one horse, and that was enough.

CHAPTER 21

"SADDLE BAGS ARE PACKED. WHO WANTS them?"

"Huh!" Brooke jumped slightly as Dad appeared beside her at the hitching rail. After the strained silence of the past few minutes, the sound of his voice had startled her. She turned to see if Skye wanted to take the bags. In response, Skye raised three fingers and pointed at Jazz. Speechless, Brooke shook her head lightly. Clearly Skye had only one thing on her mind, and that was Morris. Why else would she insist that Brooke lead the horses out on her own? She did not seem to understand that Brooke wanted to ensure all the horses made it home safely. The best way to do that was for them to ride out together.

Dad held up the leather bags. "Nobody wants these?"

Brooke stared as Skye turned her back and mounted up on Indee. When it was obvious she wasn't going to volunteer to take them, Brooke offered, "I guess I will."

Dad tied the saddle bags onto the back of her saddle. "Don't sound so excited. You'll be glad you have this food once you've been riding for a while." He reached out and untied Chocolate from the hitching rail. "You girls have a good ride. Just stick together and keep to the road. You shouldn't have any problems."

Brooke climbed into the saddle and reached down to take Chocolate's rope that Dad handed to her. Stick together and have a good ride? That seemed highly unlikely unless Skye's chilly mindset melted after a few miles on the road. Leading Chocolate, she began to make her way out of camp but stopped when Skye paused at the pickup.

"I'll be home as soon as I can," Skye reassured Morris, rubbing the end of his sausage-like nose. He struggled to stand up, but then toppled back down. "Don't worry, boy," she spoke soothingly. "Dad tied your legs with that rope so you wouldn't jump out of the truck while they are driving. He'll take it off when you get home."

Dad joined them. "And I'll do my best to make sure that he is still there when you get home. Tuffy can keep him company. They seem to be pretty good friends." He opened the tailgate, and Tuffy jumped inside. A few minutes later, the pickup rumbled out of the camp.

As they followed the truck, Brooke was not surprised when Indee started to prance down the road. A horse could sense how its rider was feeling, and Indee was definitely reflecting Skye's agitation.

"Are you coming or what?" Skye snapped. "If you go any slower, I could walk backwards and still be ahead of you."

Brooke bit the inside of her lip to keep from saying something she shouldn't. A war of words wouldn't benefit anyone. Perhaps if she kept pace with Skye, they could have some peace. Looping Chocolate's rope around the saddle horn so he would keep up, Brooke cued Jazz into a trot. As the minutes passed, she found that the up and down motion helped keep her warm in the chilly wind.

A short time later, Brooke was surprised to see Skye and Indee stop. She brought Jazz and Chocolate to a halt beside them.

"I've been watching those clouds," Skye pointed. "They're coming our way fast. I doubt we'll make it home before they reach us."

Brooke tucked her chin down into her coat as the wind's icy fingers swirled around her. Looking toward the dark band that framed the open valley in front of them, she saw a bolt of light flash across the clouds, turning them silver for an instant. Thunder rumbled a few seconds later. The distant storm she had heard in the early morning was not so far-off anymore.

"You're right," Brooke said as Jazz pawed at the ground and then tossed her head up and down. "Even Jazz agrees. Let's keep moving. The sooner we get home, the better."

Skye pointed a second time. "Brooke, what about that trail? If we took it we might get home before the rain hits us."

Brooke's gaze followed Skye's finger to the path she indicated. It was a narrow deer trail that rose sharply from the riverbed, leveling out about one hundred feet above their heads. From there, it wound its way along the hillside, following a ledge that disappeared into a small grove of spruce trees. Beyond the trees, she was unable to see where the trail led since at that point, the river curved sharply to the left and hid the hillside from her sight. In the distance, where the river wound its way back to the right, Brooke thought she saw a pencil thin trail that gradually traced its way to the top of the hill.

"Do you think it would work?" Skye persisted.

Brooke glanced at the blue-gray tower of clouds rolling toward them at an alarming speed and then back to the trail. From what she could see, the trail appeared passable, but what was on the other side of those trees?

"Well?" Skye demanded.

Weighing the choices in her mind, Brooke answered, "I doubt we will make it home before the storm hits us, but if we take the path we may not be in the rain for as long a time." She paused, and then said, "Sure. Let's go. The sooner we get home, the better."

"Oh, good. I'll lead." Skye gave Brooke a half-smile and turned Indee up the trail.

Brooke unwound Chocolate's rope from the saddle horn and followed Skye up the steep incline. It would be more difficult to lead Chocolate on this trail because he would have to follow directly behind Jazz instead of beside her. If the lead rope became trapped under Jazz's tail or if Chocolate didn't stay on the same side of the trees as her, they would have a tangled mess.

As they walked into the small grove of trees, Brooke warned, "Skye, don't get too far ahead." They were entering the part of the trail that she had been unable to see from the road. Skye gave her a small wave as she disappeared around a corner in the trail.

Brooke ducked her head to avoid hitting a branch. The spruce needles lightly brushed her coat as she guided the horses down the path. The towering vegetation blocked out much of the daylight, making it more difficult to see. As she scanned the ground for obstacles, she saw a flicker of movement out of the corner of her eye.

In a flash, Jazz leaped forward. Brooke lost hold of Chocolate's rope as a grey shadow flew upwards from the ground and into a tree. Jazz snorted and turned sideways, eyeing the tree with suspicion.

Brooke drew in a shuddering breathe and exhaled. Staring into the branches of the tree that stood between Jazz and Chocolate, she saw a bird sitting on some twigs, partially hidden from view. Reaching forward to rub Jazz's mane, she soothed, "It's only a little prairie chicken. He's probably more scared than you are." Directing Jazz to walk past the tree she continued, "I know you don't want to go back, but we need to get Chocolate's rope so he doesn't get away." Jazz stepped cautiously, keeping one eye on the chicken as they made their way past.

"Whoa, boy. Easy, boy," Brooke whispered. Chocolate stood motionless, eyes wide with fright. Her hand trembled as she stretched out her arm to snag the lead rope that hung limply from his halter. Just a few more inches and she'd have it, and they could continue on their way.

"Chocolate, no!" Brooke screamed as he sprang to life and bolted down the trail, spooked by the peel of thunder that roared through the valley just then. Jazz leaped forward, struggling to follow. "Oh no you don't," Brooke uttered firmly, pulling back on the reins to keep her from charging uncontrollably down the path. Jazz reared into the air, tossing her head from side to side as she fought against the bit. Brooke pulled her head to the right and turned her in tight circles to get her back under control. Looking over her shoulder, she saw Chocolate disappear around the same corner Skye had a few minutes earlier. Hopefully she would be able to catch him.

"Okay, girl. Nice and easy." Brooke released the tension on the right rein so that Jazz could continue down the trail. She pulled on the bit with her mouth, desiring to go faster, but Brooke held firm, steady pressure on both reins. She wasn't going to risk another runaway horse. As she rounded the corner on the trail, Brooke hoped to see Skye on Indee, leading Chocolate.

"What happened?" she squawked, totally unprepared for the sight before her eyes.

Skye was in a crumpled heap on the ground.

And no horses were in sight.

CHAPTER

22

SKYE PICKED HERSELF UP OFF THE ground. "What happened?" she sputtered, her face red with rage. "I heard you yell, so I turned Indee around. The next thing I knew Chocolate rammed into us, knocking Indee to his knees and sending me into a nosedive. Indee didn't wait around. He got up and chased after Chocolate, hot on his heels."

Trying to ignore the fury in Skye's voice, Brooke questioned, "Are you hurt?" The only signs she could see of her tumble were some dried spruce needles sticking to her pants and coat.

"I'm fine, but thanks to you, two horses are running loose in the hills. One is dragging his lead rope and another his reins."

Brooke didn't hold back her temper from oozing out into her words. She had been putting up with Skye's sassiness since before they left camp. Enough was enough. "It wasn't my fault," she seethed. "A chicken spooked us."

"A chicken? Seriously! You are going to blame this on a chicken," Skye stated, sarcasm dripping like water from her voice. "And what chicken do you mean? I rode on the same path that you did, and I never saw one."

"Of course you didn't. You know that they often stay concealed while the first horse goes past, thinking they can hide. It's when the second and third horses pass by that they panic and fly away."

"Well, chicken or not, it is still your fault. If you would have held onto Chocolate more tightly, none of this would have happened."

"My fault? I could barely keep Jazz under control, let alone Chocolate. And who was the one that suggested we take this stupid trail in the first place? If we had stayed on the road like we were told none of this would have happened." Brooke was near the boiling point. If Skye said one more thing about this being her fault . . .

"Well, you could have said or done something. If anything happens to Indee, I'll . . ." Skye's shoulders slumped forward as she turned away.

Brooke's anger seeped away when she saw a tear slide down the side of Skye's face. "Look, what happened in the past is in the past. Arguing with each other about who should have done what isn't going to help us find Indee and Chocolate." She slipped her foot out of the stirrup. "Climb up behind me, and we'll follow the trail. They will probably run home, and if they do get into trouble, we should find them right away." She held the reins to keep Jazz from moving around as Skye climbed up behind her. As she had not doubled on Jazz before, she was unsure if Jazz would mind carrying two riders.

Skye wrapped her arms around Brooke's waist. "Okay, I'm on. Let's go."

When Jazz didn't put up a fuss with the extra weight on her back, Brooke directed her to continue along the trail. As they broke out of the trees, the cold, fierce wind tore past Brooke, greedily sucking the warmth out of her. She pulled her coat collar up to her ears and tucked her chin down inside. Raising her right hand to shield her eyes against the wind, she surveyed the setting before her. They were continuing to navigate the part of the trail that she had not been able to see from the bottom of the river valley, and what lay before them made her wish again they had stayed on the road.

In front of her was a narrow, deep ravine. A few brave bushes clung to the vertical sides of the cliffs, decorating the grey limestone walls with spots of green. Her eyes traveled the narrow trail that crossed the miniature canyon. It appeared to have been purposefully cut out of the rock. But why would anyone have done that? Brooke's gaze continued to follow the trail where it left the ravine and split into two branches. One branch led to a large cave on the left. The other had the appearance of a long, skinny snake winding its way along the hillside.

As Brooke directed her sight back to the narrow trail before her, her heart began to race. The path was passable, but if they slipped, they would be dashed against the rocks below. There would be nothing soft about that landing. What should they do? They could return to the road but that would waste valuable time and be tiring for Jazz, as she was carrying double the weight, or they could continue on the path and hope they didn't slip. As she contemplated the options, she was prodded in her back by a persistent finger.

Skye pointed excitedly. "Look, Brooke. There they are!"

Looking past the cave, Brooke regarded the two dark figures moving quickly along the green hillside. "It looks like they are heading for home, and neither one appears to be limping."

"C'mon, let's go," Skye urged.

Brooke pointed at the ravine and the narrow trail they would have to use to go over it. "Are you sure you want to cross that?"

"Chocolate and Indee made it, didn't they? C'mon Brooke," Skye pleaded. "Don't be such a chicken. Let's go."

Unwillingly, Brooke's eyes wandered to the bottom of the ravine. It was a long way down, but Skye was right. If Chocolate and Indee had made it, they could as well. Deciding to move forward, she said, "All right, we'll go. But make sure you keep still. We don't want to throw Jazz off balance by shifting our weight." She cued Jazz onward, trusting that she would be as sure-footed now as she had been in the past. Jazz lowered her head, walked forward, and tested the path one hoof at a time. Too petrified to look down Brooke focused on the black tips of Jazz's ears. She felt Skye's grip around her waist tighten. In spite of all her brave talk, Miss Fearless was feeling a little frightened too.

Reaching the other side, Brooke reached down and rubbed Jazz's shoulder. They had made it. Once again, her horse had come through for her. Hopefully, from this point on, the trail would be easy going. There had been enough excitement for one day.

Eager to get home, Brooke urged Jazz forward. As she raised her eyes, she saw that her hope for a calm ride was short-lived. Her troubles were far from over.

In fact, they had just gotten worse.

The valley in front of them had disappeared from sight as the dark clouds burst and a wall of rain charged straight toward them.

CHAPTER 23

INSTINCTIVELY, BROOKE KNEW THIS WAS A storm from which they had to find shelter. Tearing her eyes from the torrent of rain that would soon turn the hills into a giant waterslide, she frantically searched for a place to hide. Her gaze landed on the darkened hole in the hillside about two hundred feet ahead of them and to the left. It was perfect.

"Skye, we have to get to the cave," Brooke urged as she slid out of the saddle. She was not certain how Jazz would react once the rain hit them. If she happened to rear or spook, Brooke did not want to be thrown from the saddle. She would rather be controlling her horse from the ground.

"But what about Indee?" Skye whimpered.

"You want to try and ride in that?" Brooke pointed at the downpour that was fast approaching. Skye hesitated a moment, then jumped out of the saddle and fled to the cave.

"Wait! I need your help," Brooke said in earnest, but her cries were ignored as Skye darted inside. Turning her back to the wind, she tried to shield her face as the first drops of rain pelted her. Within seconds she was swallowed in the full fury of the storm. She reached to the back of her saddle for her rain slicker and then remembered it was still in the tack room at camp. But it didn't matter. She was already soaked through to the skin.

Drawing Jazz's head to her chest, she smoothed the dampened mane on Jazz's face. Speaking loudly to be heard above the wind, she said, "I hope you don't run away on me as well." Jazz nudged her shoulder and blew warm air on her face. Brooke gave her a quick hug, reassured that Jazz appeared to be calm in the middle of the storm. She peeked over her shoulder at the cave. Its outline was barely visible through the grayness that surrounded them. Brooke took hold of Jazz's lead rope. They had to get moving. If the storm worsened, they would not be able to see where to walk.

"C'mon Jazz," Brooke coaxed. "Let's goooooo . . . Awww!" She clung to the rope as her feet slipped on the wet rocks and she landed with a thud on her rump. She struggled to her feet and regained her balance. "Sorry about that girl. Riding boots on wet rocks are like wearing skates on ice." She tried to wipe some of the rain off of Jazz's head, but it was pointless. A small waterfall was pouring off the end of her nose.

"Let's get to the cave." Brooke pulled on the rope and hunched forward into the storm as the whipping wind and slimy ground threatened to unbalance her again. Straining to see through the water to make sure they were headed in the right direction, her heart faltered. Where was the cave?

"Skye! Help!" Brooke shrieked. She paused, struggling to catch the sound of Skye's voice over the roar of the storm. She called again, but it was impossible to hear anything but the wind and rain. Panic gripped her. A few steps in the wrong direction and she would lead herself and Jazz right off the hillside. What was she going to do?

She took a deep breath to clear her head. She had to think. Before the storm had hit, the cave had been ahead of them about 200 feet and off to the left. Since Jazz hadn't moved, she should still be facing in the right direction.

"Okay, Jazz. I'm going to need your help on this." Gripping the lead rope right under the halter Brooke took two steps. Jazz followed. Slowly, little by little, they moved forward. Lightening flashed with thunder roaring at its heels. For a split second the curtain of rain glowed with a silver light.

Brooke cheered when she saw the shadowy outline of the cave opening. "There it is, Jazz. We're headed in the right direction." Together they took several steps forward. But then, with the storm swirling around her and the rain pelting her face with a frenzy, Brooke began to feel confused and dizzy, making her uncertain they were still going in the right direction.

"Skye!" Brooke cried out. Surely Skye would hear them now. Guiding Jazz a few more steps, she called out again. This time she could distinguish the higher pitch of Skye's voice above the rumble of the storm. Following the voice like a lifeline, Brooke slowly led Jazz. This was like playing follow the leader, only she was blind and had no idea where the leader was. As the mouth of the cave became visible, Brooke ran forward. Shelter!

"Are you alright?" Skye exclaimed.

"I'm . . ." Brooke started to answer, but never finished. Her right arm shot backwards, and her feet flew out from under her. As she hit the cave floor, she heard Jazz snort behind her and felt her pull back on the rope. Frantically, Brooke swung her free hand around and struggled to grasp the rope with both hands.

"Skye, help!" Brooke could feel her fingers slipping on the wet rope. If Jazz pulled back much more, she would be free.

"Hang on!" Skye grasped at the rope. "Okay, I have her. You can let go."

Stiff with cold, Brooke struggled to her feet. As the thunder roared around them, Jazz's head flew up, her eyes wild with fear. Gaining her balance, Brooke joined Skye and struggled to get Jazz under control. What was going on? Why was she spooking about the storm now? She had been fine a few minutes ago.

Brooke took a deep breath and fought to keep the fear out of her voice. "Whoa Jazz! Easy girl!" she coaxed. She had to be calm so Jazz would have a reason to trust her. Thankfully, for the moment, that seemed to be happening. Brooke took the opportunity to make a plan with Skye.

"We've got to get her into the cave."

"How are we going to do that? She looks like she's ready to bolt."

"I don't know, but I can't lose her." If Jazz ran away in this storm she might hurt herself or worse. In her mind's eye,

Brooke could again see the images of Buckshot tumbling down the hill. She couldn't let that happen to Jazz. There had to be a way to get her inside. Pulling lightly on the rope, Brooke tried to reason with Jazz. "C'mon girl, you can do it. It's nice and dry in here. You don't have to stand out in the storm." Jazz began to move toward them, but then quickly backtracked. Her eyes were wide and her nostrils flared as she snorted into the wind.

Brooke leaned in close to Skye. "You hang on to the end of the rope. I'm going to walk slowly to her head. Maybe if I am beside her I can coax her in." Sliding one hand along the rope, Brooke left the shelter of the cave and joined Jazz in the downpour. Gripping one of the halter bands with her left hand, she put her right hand on Jazz's neck and rubbed it as she talked.

"Easy girl. It'll be alright. We just want to get you out of this storm so you will be safe." Little by little, Jazz's head came down, but as soon as Brooke put pressure on the halter to lead her forward, her head flew up again. Hanging onto the halter, Brooke struggled to see into the cave. Was Jazz sensing or smelling some creature in there? As the hole was large, any size of animal could be hiding in there, and judging by the evidence on the cave floor, evidence that animals always tended to leave behind, some had ventured inside before.

"Did you see any animals in the cave?" Brooke hollered.

"No," Skye answered. "If there were any in here, do you think I would still be standing here?"

As she continued to rub Jazz's neck, Brooke sorted her thoughts. If Jazz wasn't scared of the storm and there weren't any animals in the cave, maybe she was terrified of the cave itself. Many horses lost their wits when they had to enter a horse trailer or barn. There was something about a small, dark place that scared them; however, by giving them time to think most horses could be encouraged to go in.

"I have a plan," Brooke loudly explained. "Keep a good grip on the rope, but let it hang loose. Don't pull on it unless she tries to run away." When Skye nodded, Brooke turned her attention back to Jazz. She applied light pressure to Jazz's halter. As soon as Jazz took one step forward, she immediately released the pressure and rubbed Jazz's head, giving her a moment to think and relax. Little by little Brooke was able to coax Jazz inside the cave.

Skye handed her the rope. "I didn't think you would get her inside, but you did it."

Taking the rope, Brooke wiped the rain and a few tears from her face. The wild look in Jazz's eyes was fading as she relaxed. Brooke inhaled the damp, musty air and leaned against the hard wall of the cave. She began to tremble as waves of relief rushed over her. They had made it. They were inside the cave. They were safe.

"I . . . am . . . s-so . . . c-cold," Brooke stammered as her teeth rattled together and every muscle in her body began to quiver. Sucking in another deep breath, she tried to get them to relax, but they had a mind of their own. She sank down to the ground, brought her knees up to her chest and wrapped her arms around them. Her wet clothes were driving the coldness deep inside of her.

Skye joined her on the floor of the cave. "What I wouldn't give for some matches right now."

"Or a n-n-ice warm b-bed." Brooke huddled in close to Skye. Maybe between the two of them they would be able to generate some warmth. As another bolt of light flashed, she saw that the interior of the cave tunneled further back into the hillside. The ground trembled beneath her as thunder cracked like a whip on the heels of the lightning, echoing through the cave. Brooke clasped the lead rope tighter.

"E-easy, g-girl," Brooke said anxiously as Jazz eyed the storm. Jazz looked back at Brooke, licked her lips and breathed deeply. Reassured that Jazz was beginning to relax, Brooke loosened her grip on the rope.

"Think she's going to run?" Skye asked.

"I d-don't think so. L-looks like she p-p-prefers it in h-here."

"Do you think the storm will last long?"

"I d-don't know. The s-storm is moving f-fast, b-but it could be a b-big one." Brooke rubbed her jaw bones in an attempt to get them to relax. Carrying on a conversation with chattering teeth was not easy. "I'm g-glad we s-saw the cave b-before it hit."

"Me too," Skye agreed. "But I'm worried about Indee. He's out there somewhere." Her eyes grew large as she stood up. "What if he slips off the hillside? Or gets tangled in his reins?" Her voice rose in pitch. "He could get hurt really bad or he might even . . . he might even die." She shook her head. "I've got to go find him."

"S-stop!" Brooke yelled, her voice sounding hollow as it rang through the cave. The expression in Skye's eyes mirrored the panicked look that had just been in Jazz's eyes. Brooke struggled to stand, her cold, cramped muscles complaining with each movement. She grabbed hold of Skye's arm and pointed to the waterfall that poured over the entrance of the cave. "You can't go out in that!" Skye was often fearless, but this bordered on crazy.

The terrified look drained away, and Skye's shoulders slumped. "I know I can't go, but I'm just so scared. What if something happens to him?"

Brooke put her arm around Skye's trembling shoulders, understanding how she felt. Skye's usual confidence had given way to a fear that was causing her to act irrationally. Brooke had felt the same way for months after the accident.

Brooke led Skye away from the cave opening. It was up to her to keep them safe. "C'mon, let's go sit down," she encouraged. Once they were seated on the floor, Skye cupped her face in her hands and began to cry. Brooke gave her shoulders a squeeze and looked at the wall of water pouring over the mouth of the cave. Skye had good reason to be scared. There was zero visibility outside, and the rain would make the hills as slippery as ice. It would only take one wrong step for Indee or Chocolate to be hurt.

Or it might be worse.

They could meet their deaths somewhere on the hills.

Just like Buckshot had.

CHAPTER 24

BROOKE REACHED OVER AND NUDGED HER sister. "Skye, the rain is letting up." After she had tried to race out into the storm, Skye had slumped against the wall of the cave and eventually cried herself to sleep. Brooke looked at her watch. That had been over two hours ago. She stood up and walked to the mouth of the cave, her muscles groaning as she did. Sitting too long in one position had caused them to stiffen up, but at least she was warm.

Skye's voice crackled. "How does it look?"

"Hopeful," Brooke answered. Although there was still a small sprinkling of raindrops, she could almost see across the valley. Up in the sky, the rays of the sun were breaking through the gray mass of clouds. While she could hear the occasional clap of thunder in the distance, it appeared that the storm had passed.

Skye joined her at the entrance. "Think we can leave?"

"Not yet, but soon. We have to wait until the ground has dried enough so that Jazz won't slip while she's walking." Brooke inhaled deeply, filling her lungs with the freshly washed air. As she exhaled, a distant sound tickled her ears.

"Hey! Do you hear that? It sounds like rushing water. It must have rained enough for the river to begin flowing again." Eagerly she looked down into the bottom of the valley.

"There is no way that trickle of water is generating that much sound," Skye replied.

Brooke watched a thin stream wind its way lazily through the rocks in the river bottom. Realizing Skye was right, she questioned, "Where is that sound coming from then?" She stepped back inside the cave and listened. "Hey, it's louder in here than it was outside. Skye, why don't you follow the tunnel and see what you can find?" Brooke said eagerly. She didn't know how or why the river would be inside the cave, but it could be the key to saving the ranch.

"Me?" Skye squeaked. "I'm not going back there. If you want to check it out, you go."

"I can't leave Jazz. If she runs away, it will be a long trip home on foot."

Skye extended her hand. "Give me the rope. I will hold her."

"You will? Oh, okay." Brooke placed the rope in Skye's hand and then turned to follow the tunnel into the interior of the hillside. Nervously, she took one step after another, letting her fingers trail over the cool rock walls. Looking back to the entrance she saw that Skye watching her. It would be so easy to turn around and go back, but the thought of finding the missing water and saving the ranch gave her courage to continue. As the passageway turned to the right, the light receded and soon Brooke found herself walking in darkness. She lost all sense of time and direction. Her fingers were her eyes as they trailed along the rough crevices of the cave wall. The roar in the tunnel grew louder, and when Brooke felt the dampness of water on her face, she cried out with joy.

She had found the lost river.

Now the ranch could be saved!

Excited and relieved, Brooke turned around, impatient to get back to the ranch and tell Dad the good news.

"Umph." Brooke tripped and fell forward, landing hard on her hands and knees. What had she tripped over? Blindly, she ran her fingers over the bottom of the floor. They came to rest on what felt like a thin, smooth piece of wood. Rising to her knees, she picked it up and slowly ran her fingers along its length. At one end of it she felt a piece of metal. Judging by its shape, it felt like an axe.

"But what would an axe be doing this far inside a cave?" Brooke asked herself. It didn't make sense. Axes were used for splitting wood and there were no trees in here. Confused, she felt the metal again, letting her fingers slide over to the other end of the metal head this time. It tapered down to a thin point.

Tingles of dread and excitement shot through her fingertips and filled her heart as she realized what she had found.

It was a mining axe.

Her thoughts travelled back to the story Dad had told her that dark night. He had said no one had been able to find any trace of Old Pete or the mining axe he always carried with him.

What if this was his mining axe?

Was it possible she had found Old Pete's lost cave?

CHAPTER 25

As the interior blackness of the cave receded into gray and then into light, Brooke rushed forward. "I'm back," she announced, relieved to see Skye and Jazz still waiting at the cave entrance.

Skye turned around to face her. "Did you find it?"

Brooke nodded. "There is definitely water running back there, and look what else I found." She held out the axe.

Skye took it and turned it over in her hands. "What is an axe doing in a cave?"

"That's the same question I asked. The only thing that I could think of was that it might belong to . . ."

Skye broke in. "Old Pete?"

"How did you know?"

Skye pointed to the end of the handle. "Look here."

Brooke peered down at the axe. There were some initials carved into the wood. "P.M.?" she questioned out loud. "Didn't Dad say his name was Pete McGuire?"

"Yeah, something like that," Skye said. "Do you think it's possible that you found Old Pete's cave?"

Brooke looked back into the tunnel. "When I was back in there I was wondering if it could be. Now seeing the axe with his initials makes it seem more likely. I wonder what happened to him." Brooke paused, letting her mind wander. Had he travelled farther into the depths of the cave and been unable to get back out? Or had he made it out and left his axe behind for some reason? Brooke shook her head. That story happened a long time ago. Right now they had a ranch to save. It was time to get going. The clouds were gone, and the warmth of the sunshine was drying the ground.

Taking a hold of Jazz's lead rope, she said, "Let's go home. Just leave the axe in the cave entrance. We have to bring Dad back here, so we can show it to him then." Leading Jazz outside, she tightened up the cinches on the saddle. She climbed up, waited as Skye got on behind her, and then turned Jazz up the trail.

"Brooke! Skye!" A voice ricocheted back and forth across the hills.

Looking down into the valley, Brooke saw Dad on Chocolate, galloping hard along the road. "Dad!" she yelled.

Chocolate slid to a stop, and Dad looked around.

"Up here!" she called again.

Dad spotted them and waved. "What are you doing up there?"

"We . . ." Brooke stopped. The story was too complicated to explain it while yelling. Dad would have to come to where they were. "Go upriver," she instructed. "You will find the trail."

As Dad disappeared, Brooke climbed out of the saddle and looked up at Skye, "Did you notice who Dad was riding?"

Skye slid to the ground with a big smile. "Yes. I hope that means Indee made it home too."

Sometime later Brooke saw Dad break out of the trees on the other side of the ravine.

"Did you cross this?"

"Yes," Brooke answered, and she watched Dad make his way across on the narrow path. Now that she had found the mining axe, she understood why the path appeared to be carved out of the rock. Old Pete must have made it.

Dad rode onto the scene and slid to the ground. He gave both of them a big hug. "What on earth happened? Indee showed up at home with no rider, and Chocolate wasn't far behind. When Jazz didn't come, I was sure something bad had happened. As soon as the rain let up a little, I rode out."

"Indee made it home?" Skye's voice was almost a whisper.

"Yes. He's safe and sound, enjoying a good meal of oats in the barn."

Brooke proceeded to give Dad all the details about what had happened, leaving out the part about the arguing and how Skye had acted when she got scared.

"It's a good thing you had Skye here to help you," Dad commented. "Sounds like you had your hands full with Jazz being so scared."

"I didn't do very much, Dad," Skye admitted. "In fact, Brooke kept me from doing some pretty stupid things. She was really brave. It was because of her that we were all safe inside the cave through the storm."

Surprised at Skye's admission, Brooke looked her way and whispered, "Thank you."

Skye nodded back and smiled.

"Skye, could you hold Jazz? I want to show Dad the cave." She gave Skye the reins and then led Dad into the cave.

"Listen," she directed.

Dad was quiet. His eyes grew large. "Is that what I think it is?"

Brooke nodded. "I followed the tunnel and found water flowing in there. And look what else I found." She handed him the axe and pointed to the initials.

Dad peered at it. "P. M. Old Pete?"

"That was our guess."

"Wow, Brooke! That is amazing. Not only did you look after Jazz and Skye in the storm, but you solved the mystery of the lost river and found a clue to the disappearance of Old Pete. Looks like my little girl is growing up and becoming a first-rate ranch hand at the same time." Dad put his arm around Brooke's shoulder. "C'mon, let's go home."

Brooke beamed at Dad's words as they walked outside. He thought she was a first-rate ranch hand! Unable to contain her delight, she gave Dad a big bear hug. Stepping back, she asked, "Do you have any idea how the water got into the cave?"

Dad shrugged his shoulders. "I don't know. Limestone is a soft rock, so it could be that the river somehow cut a new channel for itself that led it underground."

"But how will we get the water out?"

"We will need to find where it disappears underground. Once we discover that, we can develop a plan of how to get the water back to the river on a long term basis. For the short term, we can bring a gas-powered water pump, some fuel, and long hose to the cave so we can pump some of the water back to the river." Dad looked at Brooke. "I still can't believe you found the water. I was really worried we wouldn't find it. You saved the ranch, Brooke."

Brooke couldn't stop her smile as she climbed onto Jazz. Although they still had a couple of hurdles to cross, hopefully now the ranch would be able to continue as it had for so many years already.

Skye walked up and tapped her on the leg. "Since I am still horseless, can I ride with you?"

"Sure, get on." Brooke waited while Skye climbed up and then followed Dad up the trail toward home.

"Hey, Dad. Is Morris still at home?" Skye wondered.

Dad looked back over his shoulder. "Yup. He and Tuffy were warm and dry in the barn. And when it started to rain, the vet and game warden called to say they wouldn't be coming until tomorrow."

"Yes." Brooke heard Skye whisper behind her, and she was happy for her. A light wind blew wisps of hair across Brooke's face, tickling her nose. She pulled out the band that held her hair in a ponytail and stared at the fluorescent pink elastic. After all the excitement of the past few days, she still had the same one Skye had given her.

"What did you say the color pink means?" she asked.

"Friendship," Skye replied.

Thoughtfully Brooke tied her hair back in a ponytail. A friendship elastic. It was a good symbol of the bond she shared with Skye. As sisters, their relationship would always be stretching and growing. Just like they had experienced over the past few days, there would be rough spots and times when their friendship was challenged, but through it all they would stick together.

Not only as sisters, but also as friends.

As they continued along the trail, Brooke relaxed as the warmth of the sun soaked into her. She was thankful they had survived the storm; the ranch was safe, and she still had her horse. Reaching forward to rub Jazz's neck, she realized that it took a good deal of courage to be a cowgirl. She would never know what she might encounter, but as long as she didn't let fear take hold of the reins, she could have the courage to take action. Courage didn't mean she would never be afraid. It just meant that she could be brave in the face of fear.

That's the kind of courage she wanted to have.

A cowgirl's courage.

CPSIA information can be obtained at www.ICGtesting.com
Printed in the USA
LVOW12s0911191113

361851LV00001B/3/P